"Noname's" Latest and Best Stories are Published in This Library.

FRANK READE LIBRARY

Entered as Second Class Matter at the New York, N. Y., Post Office, October 5, 1892.

No. 25. {COMPLETE.}  FRANK TOUSEY, PUBLISHER, 34 & 36 NORTH MOORE STREET, NEW YORK. {PRICE 5 CENTS.} Vol. I
New York, March 11, 1893.  ISSUED WEEKLY.

Entered according to the Act of Congress, in the year 1893, by FRANK TOUSEY, in the office of the Librarian of Congress, at Washington, D. C.

# Frank Reade Jr.'s New Electric Terror the "Thunderer;"
## OR, THE SEARCH FOR THE TARTAR'S CAPTIVE.

By "NONAME."

# FRANK READE
## Adventures in the Age of Invention

**PAUL GUINAN**
*and*
**ANINA BENNETT**

AUTHORS OF **BOILERPLATE**

Abrams Image – New York

The authors extend their deepest appreciation to the Frank Reade estate for cooperating in the preparation of this book. The Smithsonian, Library of Congress, and Oregon Motor Museum are also remarkable resources. Thanks go out to David Hahn, James Sinclair, Sean Guinan, Ben Dewey, Kathy Oleson, and the lovely Claire Hummel for their contributions. And a special tip of the hat to Joe Rainone, who provided access to his unparalleled collection of *Frank Reade* dime novels.

EDITOR

**DAVID CASHION**

DESIGNER

**MARTIN VENEZKY'S APPETITE ENGINEERS**

PRODUCTION MANAGER

**JACQUIE POIRIER**

LIBRARY OF CONGRESS CATALOGING-IN-PUBLICATION DATA

Guinan, Paul.
Frank Reade : adventures in the age of invention / Paul Guinan and Anina
Bennett.
p. cm.
ISBN 978-0-8109-9661-8 (alk. paper)
1. Robots—Comic books, strips, etc. 2. Graphic novels. I. Bennett,
Anina. II. Title.
PN6728.G769F73 2012
741.5'973—dc22
2011009742


ISBN: 978-0-8109-9661-8

PRINTED AND BOUND IN CHINA
10 9 8 7 6 5 4 3 2 1

THE ART OF BOOKS SINCE 1949
115 WEST 18TH STREET
NEW YORK, NY 10011
WWW.ABRAMSBOOKS.COM

# FRANK READE

## WEEKLY MAGAZINE,

### Containing Stories of Adventures on Land, Sea & in the Air.

Issued Weekly—By Subscription $2.50 per year. Application made for Second-Class Entry at N. Y. Post-Office.

No. 19.          NEW YORK, MARCH 6, 1903.          Price 5 Cents.

SIX WEEKS IN THE CLOUDS;

OR, FRANK READE, JR.'S AIR-SHIP THE "THUNDERBOLT".

BY "NONAME."

At this moment the Klamaths burst out of the cavern. But they had come just too late. Frank Reade. Jr., was in the pilot house, and the airship shot upward into the zenith.

# INTRODUCTION

WELCOME to the Age of Invention—the nineteenth century, when human ingenuity brought forth an unending stream of revolutionary technology, such as electric lights, telephones, automobiles, refrigeration, airships, and robots. When there were still huge swaths of uncharted territory on Earth and in science. When anything seemed possible.

Even against this fantastic backdrop, one family stands out as the most ingenious, intrepid adventurers of the era: Frank Reade and the two generations of descendants who followed him. From the 1870s through World War I, they were celebrities, renowned as "distinguished inventors of marvelous machines in the line of steam and electricity." As friends of Archibald and Lily Campion, they crossed paths with Archie's famous robot, Boilerplate, on more than one occasion.

Best known for inventing helicopter airships and early robots called the Steam Men and Electric Man (which predate Boilerplate), the Reades—especially Frank Reade Jr.—traveled all over the planet. Their globe-trotting exploits captured the public imagination and became the basis of popular dime novels that ran for decades.

Millions of readers thrilled to Frank Jr.'s fictional adventures, eagerly awaiting each new issue of *Frank Reade Library* or *Frank Reade Weekly*. The plots ranged from the familiar to the fantastic, from fighting bandits in Mexico to discovering lost races and riding comets into outer space. Many of the elaborate illustrations from these stories, forgotten pieces of Americana, have been painstakingly restored and are reprinted in this volume for the first time in a century.

The prolific Reade clan also designed an amazing array of electric all-terrain vehicles, electric weapons, and submarines, all far ahead of their time. Even their hometown of Readestown, Pennsylvania, bore their name, and its economy revolved around their Readeworks manufacturing business. Although Readeworks no longer exists, another branch of the family operates Reade Chemicals in New York.

Until recently, this was all that was publicly known about Frank Reade and his progeny. Today, they seem like mythic figures, frozen icons of a bygone time. But their personal journals and correspondence, declassified by the U.S. Office of Naval Intelligence in 1997, reveal a more nuanced—and more human—picture. It is a story of generational conflict, international intrigue, hubris, charity, regret, and redemption. In it, we can see the birth of modern technology, politics, and business, writ large in the lives of a remarkable family.

# FRANK READE

## WEEKLY MAGAZINE,

### Containing Stories of Adventures on Land, Sea & in the Air.

Issued Weekly—By Subscription $2.50 per year.    Application made for Second-Class Entry at N. Y. Post Office.

No. 48.        NEW YORK, SEPTEMBER 25, 1903.        Price 5 Cents.

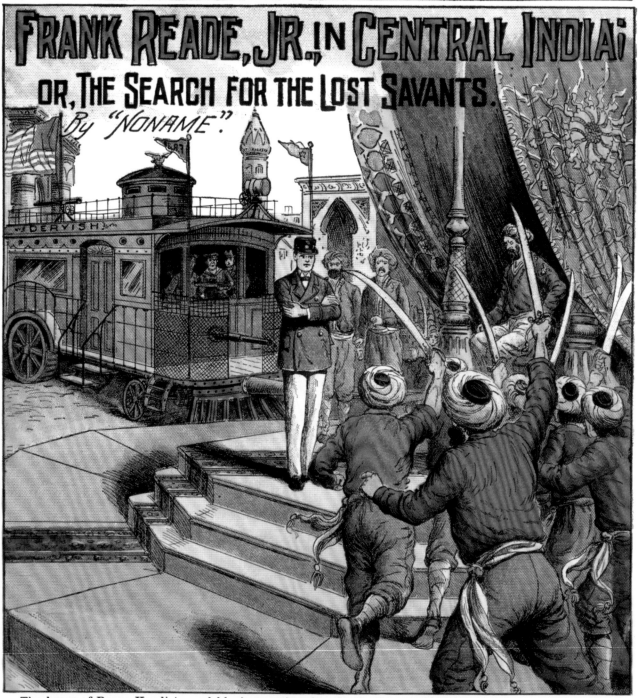

# FRANK READE, JR., IN CENTRAL INDIA
## OR, THE SEARCH FOR THE LOST SAVANTS.
### By "NONAME."

The brow of Rassa Hendi turned black as a thunder-cloud.  The rumble of war-drums sounded upon the air, and the Sayk soldiers rushed upon the dais with drawn swords and savage mien.  The situation looked critical for Frank.

# AGE *of* CHANGE

THE WORLD KNEW MY PAPA AS A LEGEND: *genius inventor, bold explorer, rescuer of innocents, vanquisher of villains. My brother and I knew him as the father who lived with us in between his audacious adventures, and who at times took us on fantastic voyages, but whose life was half a mystery. In truth, none of us fully knew the man whose journal I'm reading now—maybe not even Papa himself.*

JOURNAL OF KATE READE (JANUARY 7, 1933)

## OUT *of the* PAST

IN 1932, Kate Reade stumbled across her father's journal and a trove of family letters dating back to the mid-1800s. Although he didn't pen many letters himself, it turns out Frank Reade Jr. was more sentimental than anyone suspected.

*Magazine ad for the Frank Reade dime novels.*

❦     *I was perusing Papa's personal hoard of old blueprints—he never would let anyone else keep copies of the final plans for his inventions, not even* [Readeworks foremen] *Jack Wright or Electric Bob—when I found a stout, ancient wooden trunk fitted with an electric lock. No one but Papa could've dreamt up that lock. I finally cracked it after 3 days and 2 sleepless nights.*

*And there it all was. Papa's secret journal, every letter ever sent to him (including a few from me that I'd just as soon forget about—what a twerp I was in the aughts!), and Grams' and Gramps' scribblings too. The inside dope on our family.*

*What a shocker! Papa's journal is full of stories and thoughts that I'll bet he never told anyone.*

KATE READE, LETTER TO LILY CAMPION
(DECEMBER 12, 1932)

Over the next few years, Kate combed through her father's papers, writing about them in notes, letters to friends such as Alice Roosevelt and Texas Guinan, and her own journal. She grew obsessed with answering one question: Who was Frank Reade Jr.? To shed some light on the answers, we have to go back a generation.

Frank Reade Jr. in the 1880s.

The private papers of Frank Jr., discovered by his daughter after his death.

## — YOUNG GUN —

**H**IS FATHER, FRANK READE SR., was born on the eastern edge of Pennsylvania to an Irish-German immigrant couple who lost their farm to foreclosure. In 1846, a ragtag young Frank, looking to be about six years old, showed up on his uncle Karl's doorstep in St. Louis, with a note from his mother.

➤ *My brother, I am entrusting to you my only son. I pray you to give him shelter and sustenance. He can work for it—our little man is quite handy with any sort of mechanical device.*

KATARINE ROOSA READE, LETTER TO KARL ROOSA, TRANSLATED FROM GERMAN (MARCH 22, 1846)

"Quite handy" turned out to be quite an understatement. Frank was a mechanical whiz kid. Despite his lack of formal schooling, he blazed through every science book he could get his hands on.

At thirteen, he became an apprentice in the workshops of Mississippi River salvage expert and diving bell pioneer James B. Eads. After the American Civil War broke out, Frank helped Eads design and build armored gunboats—the latest thing in naval warfare. It was the first step in the Reade family's long association with the United States Navy.

➤ *Be not surprised if you are called here* [to Washington, DC] *suddenly by telegram. If called, come instantly and bring along your young engineer, Mr. Reade. In a certain contingency it will be necessary to have the most thorough knowledge of our Western rivers, and the use of steam on them.*

U.S. ATTORNEY GENERAL EDWARD BATES, LETTER TO JAMES B. EADS (APRIL 17, 1861)

Frank Reade Sr. at the start of the Civil War.

Frank Sr. designed and built several ships that were part of the Western Gunboat Flotilla during the Civil War, including Admiral Porter's flagship *Benton* (seen in foreground). Frank Sr. was aboard the *Benton* as technical advisor during the siege of Vicksburg in 1863.

James B. Eads inspired Frank Sr. to build ironclad ships and, later, large-scale public works such as the Eads Bridge.

## — IRONCLAD VICTORY —

**N**OT CONTENT with just making the boats that would help win the war, Frank also seized his one chance to command a U.S. Navy vessel. He served as civilian captain of the USS *Dauntless* in the Battle of Memphis, which helped the Union gain control of the Mississippi River and cleave the South in half. By this time, Frank had fallen in love with and married a young lady née Mary Upchurch.

*Doubtless our conduct of the battle was hampered by inexperience and disorganization. Nevertheless we gave that Rebel fleet a sound drubbing, such that the river and the city are ours. Of their eight boats, only one has escaped capture or sinking.*

*I should like to examine the hull of a prize, for word has it these "cottonclads" are stuffed with a stratum of cotton betwixt two bulkheads. This planted in my mind the germ of a new notion—such a double-hulled construction could be useful for submersible or aerial vessels.*

*Forgive my divagation into the theoretical. I promise you, there is scarce room in my mind for thoughts of any but you—My own sweet Mary!—since the battle ended and I received your letter of 13 May. You have made me happier than a man could hope to be during wartime.*

*God willing, I shall be back at your side before the birth of our child.*

FRANK READE SR., LETTER TO MARY READE
(JUNE 10, 1862)

Frank Jr. c. 1870.

## — THE LOST YEARS —

**M**UCH TO Mary's delight, Frank made it back to St. Louis in one piece. That's where Frank Jr. was born on July 1, 1862.

The family's life was peaceful for a time, even as the Civil War raged on through the Battle of Gettysburg and Sherman's scorched-earth march across Georgia. These names still reverberate in America's memory as cataclysmic events, but for the fortunate young Reades, they were distant abstractions.

After the war, the couple moved, abruptly, to Pennsylvania. In the pastoral Delaware River Valley, where Frank Sr. had spent his early childhood, he set up his own company called Readeworks.

For Kate Reade, looking back on her family's history seventy years later, this brief period presented a tantalizing enigma.

*Odd. Just noticed a four-year gap in Papa's memory box, and I'm stumped. There's no record whatsoever from 1864–1868, not a jot or tittle, not a scrap of paper about the end of the War of Rebellion or the founding of Readeworks. What happened in those years? Why'd they leave St. Louis?*

JOURNAL OF KATE READE (JANUARY 18, 1933)

The shocking answers, when she finally found them, would be among Kate's last discoveries. ✩✩

Mary Reade in the 1870s.

Frank Reade Sr.'s captaincy of the *Dauntless* during the Battle of Memphis on June 6, 1862, was the last time the U.S. Navy officially allowed civilians to command military ships in combat. The Reades would continue their relationship with the navy for generations as private contractors.

# FULL STEAM AHEAD

**A**T FIRST Readeworks made portable steam engines, which powered all kinds of heavy equipment for manufacturing, construction, mining, and transportation. Frank Sr.'s engines were more advanced than anything else on the market, outstripping the competition in efficiency and sheer toughness. Soon business was booming, and by 1868 the company had so many employees that the settlement around it was incorporated as Readestown.

As soon as Frank Jr. got his hands on the equipment at Readeworks, it was plain to see that the son was even more of a mechanical prodigy than the father. At ten years old, he was improving on Frank Sr.'s steam engine designs. But Mary, who watched over Junior at home, was worried.

Frank Reade Sr. had early success with his portable steam engines in the timber industry.

❧ *Frank advises that we must not be overly anxious about Junior. I cannot find it within myself to set aside my worry. The boy rarely speaks, and he gazes off at phantoms we do not see. His favored pastime is to build elaborate miniature replicas of famous battles. I am heartened, however, by our son's interest in his father's workshops and machinery.*

JOURNAL OF MARY READE (MARCH 19, 1868)

## —— FRANK'S FIRST GUNSHIP ——

AROUND THIS TIME, two experiences in particular sparked Junior's curiosity and made a lasting impression on him. The first was when his father took him to see a demonstration of a steam-powered automaton—an awe-inspiring sight for a young boy, and one that stayed with Frank Jr. for life.

❧ *Never will I forget the first time I laid eyes on a mechanical man—Dederick's crude old Steam Man. Even as a child, I recognized it as a mere rudimentary first step, but in it I glimpsed the future.*

FRANK READE JR., LETTER TO
ARCHIBALD CAMPION (JUNE 20, 1893)

Frank Sr.'s *Bellona*, docked on the Delaware River near Philadelphia in the early 1870s.

The other experience was helping his father build the gunship *Bellona*. Frank Sr. hoped to win a new shipbuilding contract with the U.S. government, but the postwar navy was in decline and didn't have the budget for new high-tech vessels.

❧ *Although I regret that our Navy is so diminished in scope and ambition, Frank Junior is delighted that he will not be parted from his beloved* Bellona. *Two days past, he clambered into the ship unnoticed and endeavored to pilot it himself. He might have succeeded, but for the fact that he is too small to reach all the control mechanisms.*

*Rather than voyaging down the river according to his plan, he steered the vessel on a circular course and arrived back at its origin point. There it collided with the dock, causing no small merriment among the men. The* Bellona *is undamaged, but I cannot say the same for my son's evidently ample pride.*

FRANK READE SR., LETTER TO KARL ROOSA
(MARCH 3, 1869)

**HE IS HERE!**
THE WONDERFUL
**STEAM MAN!**

IS NOW ON EXHIBITION,
FOR A FEW DAYS ONLY,
—AT—
No. 709 South Second Street,
COMMENCING
Wednesday, Feb. 17, 1869,
FROM 10 A. M. TO 10 P. M.

This Machine has been exhibited in New York, Boston, Chicago and other large cities, in the largest halls, and run over the principal race courses, and in after the same pattern as the one now creating such a great sensation in Paris

HE PULLS A CARRIAGE
**A MILE IN 2:15!**
And performs other wonderful and almost human feats. His remarkable portrayals of
**SPEED AND POWER**
Will continue in this city for a few days, to afford
RICH THEMES FOR AMUSEMENT.
This machine has been visited by the most scientific men in the world, and pronounced by all
THE GREATEST INVENTION of the AGE.
Ladies especially should witness this
Wonderful Exhibition.
**HE WILL BE SHOWN in MOTION.**

In the years after this inaugural tour of the original Steam Man, almost a dozen other mechanical men would be demonstrated around the country, including some built by the Reades.

The *Bellona* was the last steam-powered ship made by the Reades. It was retired in 1876, replaced by the electric gunboat *Centennial*.

## "MAN HAS MADE THE WORLD SMALLER"

**R**EADEWORKS developed a brisk trade with California and the western territories— which, at the time, were practically as far away and hard to reach as the Moon. There were few paved roads, no highways, no automobiles or airplanes. Long-distance travel and shipping were grueling, slow, and expensive.

That was about to change forever. In 1869, Frank Sr. witnessed the joining of two railroad lines that knit together the continent, from the Atlantic to the Pacific Ocean. On May 10, the Central Pacific Railroad was ceremonially connected with the Union Pacific Railroad in Utah. Frank Sr. was invited to the event by a Readeworks customer, David Hewes, who owned steam shovels and was a big booster of the Central Pacific.

➤ *Thus begins a new age. I am astounded by the realization that distance is now so thoroughly annihilated—or perhaps our horizons so rapidly expanded—that man has made the world smaller.*

*No longer will the journey from eastern to western seaboard of our nation be measured in months. Imagine, a letter from your friend Lizzie in San Francisco or my client in the* *Utah Territory could reach our doorstep within a week! The transport of goods and livestock shall similarly be speeded, and I predict that we shall soon see not only increased trade, but also increased settlement within this country.*

*I hope our little "Apache" is not giving you much trouble during my absence. Tell Junior that if he behaves himself and helps you mind the house, I shall bring him a gift all the way from California.*

FRANK READE SR., LETTER TO MARY READE (MAY 11, 1869)

☆☆

Although the distance from America's East Coast to the Pacific Ocean is vast, railroads helped the United States fulfill its Manifest Destiny and settle the West.

Locomotives of the Union Pacific and Central Pacific meet at Promontory Summit, Utah, in 1869. The driving of a golden spike marked the completion of the first transcontinental railroad in the United States. It was also the nation's first live media event: The spike was wired to telegraph lines, which sent a signal to San Francisco and New York when the hammer struck.

Frank Reade Sr. is just left of center, behind the fellow holding out the bottle of champagne. Not seen are the thousands of Chinese laborers who made it all possible. California governor Leland Stanford admitted, "Without the Chinese it would have been impossible to complete the Western portion of this great national highway."

# REIGN
## of the
# RAILROADS

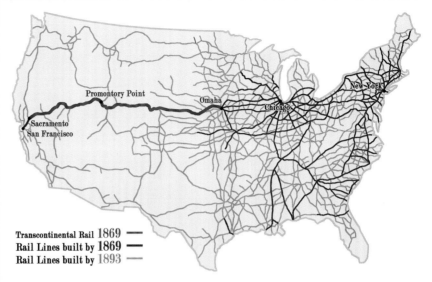

Transcontinental Rail **1869** ——
Rail Lines built by **1869** ——
Rail Lines built by **1893** ——

"**A**NNIHILATION OF SPACE" was a buzz phrase in the nineteenth century, an expression of people's profound shock as distance seemed to be collapsed by technology. In the United States, large-scale railroads—not just the trains and tracks, but the companies and the men who ran them—transformed everything.

◆ *[R]ailroads bring the produce of the country and the markets of the country in close proximity. The real distance between New York and Philadelphia, for example, is just the same now as it was a hundred years ago—but the relative distance is changed from seven days to seven hours . . . so much is space annihilated by steam.*

"THE INFLUENCE OF RAILROADS IN DEVELOPMENT OF THE RESOURCES OF THE STATE," *AMERICAN RAILROAD JOURNAL AND MECHANICS' MAGAZINE*, VOL. VII, NO. I (JULY 1, 1841)

In 1860, there were 30,000 miles of railroad track and thirty-one million people in the United States. Over the next thirty years, those numbers leapt to 270,000 miles of track and seventy-six million people. Immigrants poured into the new nation and spilled out across its western lands.

◆ *Railroads in Europe are built to connect centers of population, but in the West the railroad itself builds cities. Pushing boldly out into the wilderness, along its iron track villages, towns, and cities spring into existence.*

HORACE GREELEY ET AL., *THE GREAT INDUSTRIES OF THE UNITED STATES* (J. B. BURR & HYDE, 1872)

## —— BIG MONEY ——

**C**ORPORATIONS got bigger, too, upsized to match the massive new geographic scale, financed by investment banks and stock markets that grew along with them. The word *businessman* came into parlance for the first time, as the management and ownership of corporations got farther away from the workaday world.

Railroad companies racked up huge debts to build ahead of demand. When they stayed solvent, railroads spurred manufacturing and economic growth; when they defaulted on loans, it could touch off an international depression.

◆ *Tom Scott, whom you may recall from his tenure as Assistant Secretary of War, has made me a gift of shares in his Pennsylvania Railroad. I am grateful but as yet unaccustomed to the notion of money itself generating more money—the businessman's method.*

FRANK READE SR., LETTER TO JAMES B. EADS (MARCH 22, 1875)

A "LIMITED EXPRESS."
"Five seconds for Refreshments"!

A WILD CAT TRAIN.
No Stop Overs.

With faster transportation came a new emphasis on speed and schedules, creating scenarios like those ridiculed here. Fred Harvey opened a series of eateries along rail routes in the 1870s to service travelers with limited stopover time, thus laying the foundation for the fast-food chain restaurant.

Frank Sr., c. 1870.

This 1872 painting depicts Native Americans and wildlife fleeing as the spirit of civilization in the form of Columbia, holding a schoolbook in one hand and a telegraph wire in the other, marches west. The fate of the Indians and bison is not hinted at.

## THE DAY OF TWO NOONS

**E**VEN TIME ITSELF was altered. Until 1883, the United States was a crazy quilt of local times loosely based on the sun's position in the sky. It might be 12:30 in one town, 12:38 in the next, and 1:13 on the other side of the state. Railroad timetables, which could span dozens of local time zones, were a cryptic cascade of numbers and conversion charts.

To simplify railroad scheduling, as well as scientific observations, *standard time* was created. Train stations across the country synchronized their clocks on November 18, the Day of Two Noons. People started saying things like *on time* and *on the clock.*

◆ *The Sun is no longer to boss the job. People— 55,000,000 of them— must eat, sleep and work as well as travel by railroad time . . . The sun will be requested to rise and set by railroad time. The planets must, in the future, make their circuits by such timetables as railroad magnates arrange. People will have to marry by railroad time, and die by railroad time.*

"RAILROAD TIME,"
*INDIANAPOLIS DAILY CENTENNIAL*
(NOVEMBER 21, 1883)

★★

Frank Sr.'s pocket watch was set to "railroad time."

# GUNFIGHT at ADOBE WALLS

THE ONLY THING Junior loved more than tinkering with machinery was losing himself in adventure stories. As a child, he traveled by reading tales of Indian fighters such as Kit Carson, gold mines, pirates, secret missions, and men who explored and conquered faraway lands. These yarns—with their wildly improbable plots and titles like *The Secret Service Ship; or, The Fall of San Juan d'Ulloa*—captivated Frank Jr. and millions of other readers.

A pile of bison skulls outside Adobe Walls, which was a lucrative trading post for bison hunters in Texas and the site where Frank Jr. fought alongside Bat Masterson in 1874. The U.S. government officially encouraged the slaughter of buffalo. It weakened Native American populations by removing their main food source, cut down on railroad damage and delays caused by the herds, and opened up more rangeland for sheep and cattle.

Tales of real-life adventurers such as William Walker and Henry Morton Stanley, many of whom wrote books that exaggerated their exploits, also ranked among Frank Jr.'s favorite stories. In the young boy's mind, these men and his dime-novel heroes were cut from the same cloth.

Like Stanley, Frank Jr. himself eventually became a fusion of fiction and reality. He started early when, at twelve years old, he ran away from Readestown in search of his own western adventure. The one he found was more befitting a man twice his age.

◆ *Have no worry, I am safe in Dodge City with Bat Masterson after our glorious victory at Adobe Walls, the very same locale where Kit*

*Carson and Gen. Carleton fought off thousands of Injuns years back! We numbered only 30 men, none of us soldiers, yet our hardy band drove away some hundreds of fierce warriors of the Comanche, Kiowa, and Cheyenne. I only wish there had been Apache among them.*

*The redskins came thundering into our midst on fleet ponies, whooping and hollering, all done up in warpaint and feathers. I killed 3 of them myself, firing first a Colt revolver and then, once we had run them out of camp, a Sharps buffalo rifle. Fine weapons both.*

FRANK READE JR., LETTER TO MARY READE (JULY 28, 1874)

◆ *Young Frank Reade, who occupied half the window with me during much of the thickest of the fight, was a remarkable lad, a dead shot no matter what the distance, always alert, always looking for an opportunity to drop a bead on the enemy. When his gun spoke, his target, whether standing, walking, or running, was guaranteed to be a goner.*

BAT MASTERSON, QUOTED IN "THE BATTLE OF ADOBE WALLS," *PEARSON'S MAGAZINE*, VOL. XIX, NO. I (JANUARY 1908)

## —— HELL ON THE PLAINS ——

FRANK JR.'S PARENTS were beside themselves. Frank Sr., who had already set off for Texas in search of his son, got the news by telegram from Mary. Immediately he changed course for Dodge City, the town christened "Hell on the Plains" by a Kansas newspaper. He caught up with Frank Jr. at the Long Branch Saloon.

◆ *I found our son brandishing a glass of whiskey in one hand and a pistol in the other, regaling a crowd of roughnecks with an outlandish narrative about "shooting and chasing Injuns." He is altogether too much caught up in this frontier war and the aim of exterminating the aboriginal population (an end that may, I fear, be close at hand).*

*I write this not to cause you distress, my dear, but to emphasize the gravity of the situation. Let us send Frank overseas for a time, perhaps to London, in hopes that he may be civilized and outgrow his boyish enthusiasm for battle.*

FRANK READE SR., LETTER TO MARY READE (AUGUST 8, 1874)

Frank Sr.'s prediction of extermination didn't come true, but

Rudyard Kipling, whom George Orwell called a "prophet of British imperialism," wrote Frank Jr.'s favorite tale, *The Man Who Would Be King*. The story about two English adventurers who set off to conquer Kafiristan was adapted into a feature film starring Sean Connery.

# THE LAST CONQUERORS

**SINCE THE DAWN** of civilization, a handful of driven men have dreamt of conquering countries blessed with abundant natural resources and scant native resistance. Hernán Cortés's subjugation of the Aztec Empire showed how it was done in the seventeenth century.

But the nineteenth-century world had been mostly staked out by colonizing nations, leaving little for an individual to claim. A few ambitious men tried it anyway and, in doing so, became boyhood heroes to Frank Reade Jr.

Although Junior didn't personally take over any countries, he invaded plenty of them through the years. His adventures in and ideas about exotic lands were shaped by the writings and deeds of these men.

BROOKE

BURTON

**James Brooke** (1803–1868) started out in the private army of the British East India Company, then went into business for himself. After putting down a rebellion against the Sultan of Brunei, he was granted the title Rajah of Sarawak in 1841, establishing an English dynasty that ruled the Bornean state until 1946.

**Sir Richard Francis Burton** (1821–1890) is widely viewed as Britain's greatest explorer. Like James Brooke, he served in the British East India Company's private army, an experience he described as being "shot at for six pence a day." Burton spoke twenty-nine languages and was a knighted author, fencer, and hypnotist. His career was hindered by his writings about world sexuality and his English publication of the *Kama Sutra*, an ancient Indian text on human sexual behavior.

**Percy Fawcett** (1867–1925) was an English explorer who disappeared while looking for a lost city in the Amazon jungle. Beginning with the conquistador Francisco Pizarro centuries earlier, men had sought in vain the fabled golden metropolis of El Dorado. To distinguish his efforts, Fawcett dubbed his city *Z*. Since Fawcett's disappearance, nearly a hundred men have vanished in search of him. Only recently have archeologists found ruins in the jungle near where Fawcett was exploring.

FAWCETT

RHODES      HARLAN      WALKER

**Josiah Harlan** (1799–1871), another veteran of the East India Company's army, was an American adventurer and mercenary who traveled to Afghanistan with the intent of making himself king. He eventually became the Prince of Ghor, inspiring Rudyard Kipling to write *The Man Who Would Be King*—Frank Reade Jr.'s favorite tale.

**Cecil Rhodes** (1853–1902), a mining magnate in South Africa, amassed more than half a million square miles of land by acquiring mineral concessions from African chiefs and partnering with British colonial officials. Two Matabele Wars later, the area was officially renamed Rhodesia. Today it's known as Zimbabwe and Zambia.

**William Walker** (1824–1860) was the most infamous of all nineteenth-century *filibusters*, which is another word for a private adventurer who foments revolutions as a means of taking over foreign countries. A filibuster was considered a sort of pirate, and thus the word came to mean the hijacking of political debate. Walker succeeded in installing himself as president of Nicaragua but was quickly overthrown. He was executed a few years later, after an ill-fated attempt to take over Honduras. ★★

the end of Native American freedom in Texas wasn't far off. The second Battle of Adobe Walls touched off the Red River War, a campaign by the U.S. Army to conquer the Southern Plains tribes—Comanche, Kiowa, Southern Cheyenne, and Arapaho—and relocate them to reservations in government-designated Indian Territory. By 1875, the resistance had been broken and most of the Southern Plains tribes were confined to "the rez." ☆☆

# LONDON CALLING

**A**FTER HIS ESCAPADE as an Indian fighter in Texas, Frank Jr. was packed off to London, where his parents hoped he would stay out of trouble and cultivate a more refined character. Bringing along cousin Charley Gorse for company, he boarded with his mother's relatives and attended the City of London School. Frank Jr.'s earliest journal entries are from this period.

➤ *Oh, to be riding the Texas plains with a gun on my belt! London is too prim and proper, all rules and tradition. And yet one must admit to enjoying certain comforts such as high-class grub and furnishings.*

JOURNAL OF FRANK READE JR. (DECEMBER 5, 1874)

In London, Frank Jr. met two people who would accompany him on many an adventure: Pompei DuSable and Barney O'Shea, the school's handyman and groundskeeper. Pomp had barely escaped Mississippi when his parents were lynched after the war, while Barney was an Irishman who'd come to the City in search of work. Both men were eager learners, a quality Frank Jr. admired, and the school was progressive enough to let them use its library and even attend lectures occasionally.

➤ *I met a white boy, name of Frank, who offered me a job in Pennsylvania. He treats me like you would a smart dog, but could be he's better than most—he stopped the bobbies from locking up Barney as an Irish rebel.*

*Anyway I been wanting to come back and see how times are changing over there. I hear you got a black man in Congress and a new Civil Rights Act. Ain't no way I'm going back to Ole Miss, though. You can call on me in Readestown, Aunt Kitty!*

POMPEI DUSABLE, LETTER TO KITTY DUSABLE (MAY 29, 1875)

Pompei DuSable was Frank Jr.'s right-hand man, accompanying him on nearly every adventure, usually at the controls of a Readeworks vehicle. Pompei was not only an athlete, described by Reade chronicler Luis Senarens as "the finest horseman living," but was also capable of operating and repairing most of Frank Jr.'s machines.

From today's perspective, Frank Jr.'s attitudes about nonwhites are clearly racist. Yet the inventor considered Pompei his closest friend and trusted him with his life— which is a good thing, because Pompei saved Frank Jr.'s life on several occasions.

Pompei and his wife, Annie, at their home in Readestown. They had a son named Scipio, retired in 1919, and lived the remainder of their lives comfortably in the Pennsylvania town.

Frank Jr. in Dodge City after he took part in the second Battle of Adobe Walls. Frank Sr. was concerned enough about his son's obsession with the Indian Wars to send him overseas to "outgrow his boyish enthusiasm for battle."

Barney O'Shea was a bombastic sportsman and weapons enthusiast who also spoke French and Spanish. Although not as technically minded as Pompei DuSable, Barney served as the backup engineer aboard Readeworks vehicles during their adventures with Frank Jr.

◆ *Through thick and thin, whether dodging bullets or scaling mountains, my faithful companions were always by my side. Brothers in arms, we confronted danger in order that those at home could live in peace.*

JOURNAL OF FRANK READE JR. (SEPTEMBER 15, 1930)

✩✩

Pomp was ever hopeful about race relations in his homeland, but they would get worse—much worse—before they got better. In some ways, Frank Jr. epitomized the attitude of many white Americans: One might be friendly with a Negro, even try to educate him, yet always consider him inferior by nature.

Despite his biases, Frank Jr. came to rely on Pomp and Barney as more than friends. And although he never did outgrow his "boyish enthusiasm for battle," Frank Jr. eventually found new outlets for it.

Millions of readers thrilled to Pomp, Barney, and Frank Jr.'s many narrow escapes in the long-running *Frank Reade* dime novels.

Barney and Pomp were inseparable from the Reade family.

BARNEY

FRANK READE JR

FRANK READE

POMP

The Hon. Robert Elliott, representative from South Carolina, delivers a speech on civil rights in 1874. He was one of two dozen black congressmen in the Reconstruction era. After Reconstruction was dismantled toward the end of the nineteenth century, it would be decades before African-Americans again served in national office.

# RECONSTRUCTION

**A**FTER WINNING the American Civil War, the North tried to reshape the culture of the South through sweeping changes such as ending slavery and creating new state governments. To enforce its policies, the federal government placed the former Confederacy under U.S. Army control. Elections were held, in which freed slaves were allowed to vote and even hold political office, while ex-Confederate officials were barred from the polls.

Under Reconstruction, many Southern state governments were run by a combination of new arrivals from the North, referred to locally as *carpetbaggers*; white Southerners supporting Reconstruction, derisively called *scalawags*; and emancipated slaves, or *freedmen*. The federal government enacted new laws in an effort to enforce equality.

The inevitable backlash ranged from charges of rampant political corruption to armed opposition by groups such as the Red Shirts and the Ku Klux Klan, who used violent tactics that included torture and murder.

In the wake of the Compromise of 1877, which settled the hotly contested 1876 presidential election, federal troops were withdrawn from the South. Southerners took back political control, ending Reconstruction and passing laws that legalized segregation. Collectively called Jim Crow laws, they wouldn't be overturned for nearly a century. ★★

FOR THE SUNNY SOUTH.   AN AIRSHIP WITH A "JIM CROW" TRAILER.

A cartoon postulates how segregationist Jim Crow laws will impact future air travel.

Lynching is a form of terror used to intimidate and subdue an entire population. Thousands of blacks were killed this way after the American Civil War, including Pompei's father. Pompei himself was once almost lynched, as recounted in *Frank Reade Library* #55. Crusading journalist Ida B. Wells called lynching "our country's national crime."

**Frank Reade Library** *ran for 191 issues, and that's not even counting the other dime-novel series that starred Frank Reade Jr. and his inventions, such as* Frank Reade Weekly. *Hugely popular in their day, the stories featured a mix of realistic and fanciful elements, along with sometimes brutal violence that earned the epithet of "blood and thunder tales."*

*Excerpts from* Frank Reade Library *stories reprinted throughout this volume, such as the ones on the facing page, have been abridged and edited for readability. The rendering of Pomp's and Barney's dialects in the original versions, for example, is painfully bigoted and hard to decipher. In selecting these excerpts, it became readily apparent that the stories were written by at least two different authors. See if you can spot the differences.*

# POMP and BARNEY

*Pompei and his wife, Annie (seen at far right), arrive at a fancy-dress ball in Philadelphia.*

BARNEY

### Frank Reade Jr.'s
## "WHITE CRUISER"
#### OF THE CLOUDS; — or —
#### THE SEARCH FOR THE
## DOG-FACED MEN
*Frank Reade Library #21*

Just as the Nautchi flung Frank upon the burning pyre, the *White Cruiser* hung not four hundred feet above the clearing. Like a flash Pomp sprang to the wheel and checked the *Cruiser,* holding her directly over the spot.

Barney had leaped into the cabin, and now re-appeared with a dynamite projectile. Down he hurled it into a group of the Nautchi. The explosion was a terrific one. Dead barbarians were thrown into the air and a hole was blown in the ground big enough to sink a house in.

Down went another projectile. This time the king's throne and all in the vicinity went up in smoke.

The *White Cruiser* was swooping down like a great bird of prey. Pomp worked the gun in the turret. Shell after shell was thrown into the woods, driving away the Nautchi like frightened sheep.

Barney went over the rail and down a rope. Reaching the ground he sprang to the burning pyre and snatched Frank unharmed from it.

The air-ship rested upon the ground, the dog-faced men were routed completely, and Frank Reade, Jr., had been saved from the very gates of death.

That was a happy meeting, indeed, and all embraced with tears of joy.

### Frank Reade Jr. WITH HIS NEW
## STEAM HORSE
#### IN SEARCH OF AN
## ANCIENT MINE
*Frank Reade Library #11*

Barney rushed at Pomp with blazing vengeance. Quick as a flash, down went the darky's round wooly head. Pomp was not Barney's equal in a fist fight, but he could butt like a maddened ram. Barney received the full benefit of it full in the stomach.

*While in England, Pompei gained some notoriety as an amateur boxer, depicted here in a London sporting magazine.*

The result was comical. The Irishman's wind was completely taken away. He sat down like a thousand bricks, and giddy little aerolites and flashing planets oscillated before his bewildered vision.

### Frank Reade Jr.
## EXPLORING MEXICO
#### IN HIS NEW AIR-SHIP
*Frank Reade Library #35*

"Do they often quarrel that way?" Kensel asked of Frank.

"Once or twice on every trip," was the reply, "and Pomp head butts him out every time. They are the best friends in the world too."

"Barney is very quick-tempered."

"Yes," said Frank, "Pomp can keep his temper much better than Barney can."

"Strange they never use their weapons on each other."

"They came very near doing so once in Africa. I told them that the one who drew blood from the other with any weapon other than what nature gave them, I would shoot as I would a dog. Since that time they have never been inclined to use any weapons." **FR**

*Frank Jr. suited up for a dive, with Electric Bob, Barney, and Pompei looking on.*

# THE CENTENNIAL

**T**HE *CENTENNIAL* was the world's first electrically powered watercraft, built by Frank Sr. and his son as a prototype coastal gunboat. The vessel was originally intended to be shown at the Centennial Exhibition in Philadelphia, but wasn't finished in time. The Reades completed it later in 1876, conducting sea trials during November off the coast of Cape May, New Jersey.

The *Centennial*'s external design—a casemate ironclad with fourteen guns—was a decade old, but the 3,000 hp propulsion system was decades ahead of anything else, with a cruising speed of more than ten knots. Manned by a crew of fifty men, the vessel was approximately 300 feet in length, with a fifty-foot beam and twenty-five-foot draft. It boasted metal armor four inches thick, augmented with twenty-four inches of wood backing.

Frank Sr. began the project as a way to connect with his electrically minded son,

but also had hopes that the *Centennial* would win him a contract to build electric gunboats for the U.S. Navy. However, the navy was already struggling to make the transition from sail to steam, and its funding had been cut after the American Civil War ended. Electricity was both too new and too advanced a technology for the admirals to adopt.

Shortly after it was built, the *Centennial* did go on one mission for the navy. When a new civil war threatened to break out during the violently disputed presidential election of 1876, President Ulysses S. Grant called on Frank Sr.'s gunboat to help protect Washington, DC.

As Frank Sr. shifted his attention to large-scale public works and his son focused his seagoing interests on submarines, the *Centennial* was relegated to the dock in front of the main entrance at Readeworks. For the next twenty years, the gunboat would cruise down the

**FRANK READE** *HIS* **ELECTRIC BOAT**

Pomp and Barney atop a dime-novel rendering of the *Centennial*.

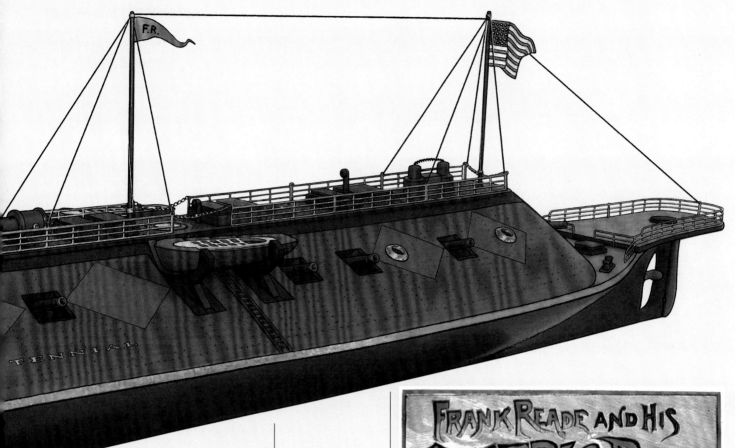

Delaware River to Philadelphia to participate in Fourth of July festivities, shooting off fireworks from the upper deck and providing cannon salutes. A few other surface vessels were produced by the Reades, but the *Centennial* remained the most famous and the family's favorite.

★★

The *Centennial* was depicted in various ways by the media. It was the beginning of a deliberate effort by the Reades to hinder attempts to copy their technology.

FRANK READE AND HIS ELECTRIC BOAT

Frank and Jesse James (standing), with Cole and Jim Younger (seated), raid the Bank of Northfield in Minnesota. The plan is Cole's, who committed the first daylight bank robberies with Archie Clement, but it goes awry this time. He and Jim are captured, while the James brothers escape.

**Little Big Horn**

Lt. Col. George Custer patrols the Black Hills because the Northern Pacific Railway arranged for the U.S. Army to protect its railroad survey. He is put on the railroad's payroll to advertise the Dakota Territory and also becomes involved in mining interests. Custer is spending so much time on business ventures that he asks for an extension of leave. The request is denied, and within months he's killed by the Sioux during the Battle of Little Big Horn.

**Deadwood**

**TERRITORIES**

**STATES**

Deadwood, inside Dakota Indian Territory, is a boomtown born during the Black Hills gold rush. This lawless town is held together by local crime boss Al Swearengen and sheriff Seth Bullock. Also in Deadwood this year are western legends Wyatt Earp and Calamity Jane.

"Wild Bill" Hickok is a celebrity gunfighter going blind from trachoma, an eye infection. On the way to Deadwood, he predicts that he'll be killed there, which suggests he's hoping to die in a gunfight. A few weeks later, Hickok is shot in the back while playing poker.

**● SAN FRANCISCO**

The Reades run an exhibition race of the Steam Man and Steam Horse in San Francisco.

# 1876
## EAST VS. WEST

**T**HE CENTENNIAL anniversary of the United States is full of events that emphasize the dichotomies of a fast-growing nation. In the crowded cities of the East, the second Industrial Revolution is going full blast, belching out pollution and chewing up immigrant workers who live in tenement slums. Meanwhile, in the West, there are still wide-open spaces, unspoiled rivers, and tribes of Native Americans living off the land.

For Native Americans of the Great Plains, a way of life that has endured for millennia will end shortly after the United States celebrates its first century.

Frank Reade Sr. salvages 70 tons of silver ore from the SS *Comet* at the bottom of Lake Superior.

New York City is the largest urban center on the continent, with a population of more than one million.

NORTHFIELD

CHICAGO

The National League's Chicago White Stockings win the baseball championship, and star pitcher Albert Spalding decides to open a store that sells his own brand of sporting equipment.

The main building of America's first official world's fair, the Centennial International Exhibition of 1876. Covering nearly 22 acres, with 75-foot-tall glass ceilings that deeply impress Walt Whitman, it's the largest structure ever built in the United States.

The Corliss Centennial Steam Engine, the largest in the world. On display at the world's fair, it's 45 feet tall, weighs more than 600 tons, produces 1,400 horsepower, and powers all the machines in the exhibition's 13-acre Machinery Hall. Frank Sr.'s Steam Man and Steam Horse are also on display.

NEW YORK

PHILADELPHIA

Elevated railroads are operating in New York City. Pedestrians occasionally get showered with embers or ash from the steam-driven locomotives above.

Alexander Graham Bell publicly demonstrates his telephone at the 1876 world's fair, generating headlines around the world. Later in the year, he demonstrates a Cambridge-to-Boston call. Within a decade, 150,000 prosperous individuals and businesses will have telephones.

Arms manufacturer Remington is selling thousands of its new Model No. 1, the first commercially produced typewriter, and first to use the QWERTY keyboard, which is the current standard configuration.

Elevators are installed in all new skyscrapers being built in major cities. Many fear the new technology, but to this day no one has ever been killed in an elevator freefall.

# THE STOLEN ELECTION

**T**HE U.S. presidential election of 1876, the most controversial in the nation's history, nearly hurled the United States into a second civil war. The Democratic candidate, Samuel Tilden, won the popular vote over his Republican opponent, Rutherford Hayes, by a quarter-million votes. The outcome looked so clear that the candidates and the country went to bed on election night believing that Tilden was the next president.

But all the returns weren't in yet, so some states' Electoral College votes were still up for grabs. In a shrewd move, around midnight, Republican stalwart Daniel Sickles sent telegrams to the Republican governors in control of three undecided states—Florida, Louisiana, and South Carolina—telling them to hold their states for Hayes. One of the replies read, "South Carolina is for Hayes. Need more troops."

A political firestorm erupted. For four months, the presidency hung in the balance. Both sides claimed victory in the disputed states, each of which submitted two conflicting sets of election results. Votes were recounted and challenged. Charges of conspiracy, vote fraud, and bribery flew in all directions. Bribes, in fact, flew in all directions.

Tensions ran so high that violence broke out in some states. "Tilden or Blood!" became an oft-heard slogan. Incumbent President Ulysses Grant, who believed Tilden had won, called up seven companies of soldiers, the USS *Wyoming*, and Frank Reade Sr.'s *Centennial* to protect the nation's capital.

Congress established a special Electoral Commission to resolve the dispute, and Republicans wound up with the deciding vote: eight to seven in favor of Hayes. Tilden took the high road and didn't press his case, much to the frustration of his followers.

Democrats objected to the Commission's decision, but agreed to accept it in a back-room deal known as the Compromise of 1877 or the Corrupt Bargain. The Republican candidate would become president in exchange for the removal of occupying federal troops and federal funding for infrastructure improvements in the South—especially railroads.

Rutherford B. Hayes, forever to be mocked in some circles as *Rutherfraud*, was sworn in as president on March 3, 1877. As Southern Democrats regained political control in their states, they dismantled Reconstruction policies and enacted segregation laws. It was a harsh setback for the four million African-Americans still living in the South. ★★

What is this in Washington shop windows, and so near Christmas?

**During the controversy that followed the 1876 election, this cartoon criticized threats of a renewed civil war as brinksmanship from politicians inured to the human cost of war. The cartoonist was the legendary Thomas Nast, who created the iconographic Democratic donkey, Republican elephant, Uncle Sam, Columbia, and modern version of Santa Claus.**

## A STAR is BORN

**A** FEW YEARS AFTER the world's fair, Junior showed signs of getting restless again, so Frank Sr. challenged his son to improve on the Steam Man II. Frank Jr. eagerly took him up on it, even wagering that it could be done in three months. Junior won the bet. One crisp September morning, a crowd gathered in the center of Readestown to watch Frank Jr. show off his new and improved Steam Man III.

Among the spectators was sixteen-year-old Cuban immigrant Luis Senarens, an aspiring writer who loved science and adventure stories. He later wrote to the young inventor with an appealing proposal: a dime-novel series starring Frank Reade Jr. and his wondrous inventions.

◆ *An excellent proposal! I agree to entertain offers from legitimate publishing houses, which should not be difficult to come by for such an exciting subject as this. Naturally any story featuring myself, any of my family, our inventions, and anyone or anything related to Readeworks must be wholly subject to my approval. I wish no unexpected revelations to be made.*

FRANK READE JR., LETTER TO
LUIS SENARENS (APRIL 24, 1880)

Together, this unlikely pair of teenagers would launch one of the best-selling entertainment franchises of their time. Senarens's first story, "Frank Reade, Jr., and His Steam Wonder," was published by Frank Tousey in 1882 in the *Boys of New York* story paper.

It was such a hit that Frank Jr. got his own titles, *Frank Reade Library* and then *Frank Reade Weekly*. Frank Sr. was featured occasionally, and there was even a spinoff series about Readeworks foreman Jack Wright. Thus they entered the ranks of other real-life figures, such as

Jules Verne, an acknowledged father of science fiction, was greatly influenced by Edgar Allan Poe and went so far as to write a sequel to Poe's *The Narrative of Arthur Gordon Pym of Nantucket.* Poe's stories were published in France as *Histoires extraordinaires (Extraordinary Stories),* and some of Verne's best-known tales collectively titled *Les voyages extraordinaires (Extraordinary Voyages).*

After Luis Senarens started writing about the Reades' Steam Men in 1879, Verne published *The Steam House* in 1880. And after Senarens printed his first account of Frank Reade Jr.'s helicopter airship in 1883, Verne's *Robur the Conqueror,* about an inventor who builds a helicopter airship, was published in 1886. Verne's sequel *Master of the World* was later made into a film starring Vincent Price as Robur.

Conceived as a friendly wager between father and son, Frank Jr.'s attempt to improve on his father's Steam Man was hailed as a success by Frank Sr.

Buffalo Bill, who became larger-than-life fictional heroes. The stories were produced and reprinted for decades, into the 1930s.

◆ *Papa never quite grew up, I think. He spent the rest of his life "chasing Injuns" in one way or another. I remember how he loved those dime novels, loved being in the spotlight but full of shadowy secrets. My famous yet enigmatic father.*

KATE READE, LETTER TO HELEN KELLER
(MARCH 11, 1934)

☆☆

Masthead for the *Frank Reade Library* series, which ran for 191 issues.

Luis Senarens was a prolific writer who penned more than 300 dime novels, some of which employ concepts that predate works by Jules Verne and H. G. Wells. The exact scope of his authorship is unknown, since many stories featuring Frank Reade or Jack Wright were written under the "Noname" pseudonym.

Senarens's output of what were then called "scientific romances" might have earned him a place in literature as a founding father of science fiction. Alas, because his stories were poorly written and published for a juvenile audience, and few of the original printings survive today, his accomplishments have been neither respected nor remembered.

# MARCH of the
# STEAM
## MEN

**A**S HAPPENS with many technologies, primitive Steam Men were developed in parallel by several minds at once. Zadoc Dederick's Steam Man, which influenced the Reades' early robotics research, was publicly demonstrated in 1868. A New Jersey newspaper described the automaton:

Zadoc Dederick invented the first Steam Man. Frank Reade Sr. purchased his patent and built a new, improved Steam Man II.

◆ *In order to prevent the "giant" from frightening horses by its wonderful appearance Mr. Deddrick [sic] intends to clothe it and give it as nearly as possible a likeness to the rest of humanity. The boiler, and such parts as are necessarily heated, will be encased in felt and woolen undergarments. Pantaloons, coat and vest, of the latest styles, are provided.*

*The face is molded into a cheerful countenance of white enamel, which contrasts well with the dark hair and mustache. A sheet iron hat with a gauge top acts as a smoke stack. Whenever the fire needs coaling, which is every two or three hours, the driver stops the machine, descends from his seat, unbuttons "Daniel's" vest, opens a door, shovels in the fuel, buttons up the vest and drives on.*

"A REMARKABLE MECHANICAL INVENTION—
A STEAM MAN," *THE NEWARK ADVERTISER*
(JANUARY 8, 1868)

Dederick's machine influenced authors as well as inventors. In 1868, Edward Ellis wrote what is arguably the first American science fiction story, *The Steam Man of the Prairies*, featuring literature's first mechanical man. That same year, another Newark inventor, Thomas Winans, constructed the Steam King, with help from Joseph Eno.

Eno went on to promote the Steam King for decades, hosting rides for dignitaries such as Ulysses S. Grant and Edward, Prince of Wales. The *Nebraska State Journal* reported that during the Modoc Indian War, Colonel George Custer took it west "as a means of frightening the hostile tribes into submission." The construct picked up the nickname "Devil Car." One of the Steam King's last appearances was at the opening ceremonies for the Queensboro Bridge in 1909.

In 1870, Enoch Morrison, inventor of the Autoperipatetikos (the first patented walking toy), created a full-scale mechanical man powered by a Behrens rotary steam engine. In 1874, Cyrenius Roe built a steam man named Adam Ironsides, and the following year a steam man toured the United States with W. W. Cole's Great New York and New Orleans Zoological and Equestrian Exposition.

At the 1876 world's fair in Philadelphia, there were no fewer than four different steam men on display, including the one built by Frank Reade Sr. ★★

Dederick's Steam Man was arguably the world's first robot. Built in 1868, it influenced fiction as well as inventors such as the Reades.

Joseph Eno's Steam King garnered more publicity than Dederick's Steam Man.

# CLEOPATRA'S NEEDLE

**F**OR HIS eighteenth birthday, Frank Jr. got to embark on an adventure that would've made his dime-novel heroes jealous. He and his father snagged a 3,300-year-old obelisk from Egypt and took it across the ocean to New York.

A few years earlier, when Britain moved a similar artifact from Egypt to London, a New York newspaper mistakenly reported that an ancient obelisk had been promised to the United States, too. The New York parks commissioner convinced railroad tycoon William H. Vanderbilt to finance an expedition to Egypt. Frank Sr.'s help was enlisted by Henry Honychurch Gorringe, a U.S. Navy colleague from the Civil War. Then it was just a question of informing the Egyptian government.

◆ *Commander Gorringe tells us the obelisk was obtained by considerable cajoling on the part of Mr. Farman, the U.S. Consul. The local populace of Alexandria is not altogether in support of this gift, and several attempts have been made to prevent its removal—one of which very nearly destroyed the artifact as it was being lowered to a horizontal position. We have therefore been obliged to alter our planned route as well as our equipment and are now engaged in floating the colossal stone obelisk on pontoons.*

FRANK READE SR., LETTER TO MARY READE
(JANUARY 20, 1880)

This trip was another formative event for Frank Jr., who had a much more politicized perspective on the situation in Egypt. He wrote about it to his new flame, Emilie Alden, an amateur astronomer.

◆ *Father thinks this a wonderful engineering project, nothing more. He doesn't ask the important questions—Who will control Egypt, its debt, its lucrative cotton trade, its new canal route to India? England or France? My British friends understand that the Khedive is but a puppet. America should make her influence felt in this region.*

FRANK READE JR., LETTER TO
EMILIE ALDEN (FEBRUARY 12, 1880)

These questions were, indeed, at the heart of international relations, then and now. But Frank Sr. was foremost interested in solving pragmatic problems such as how to safely transport a very heavy, very valuable, very old stone spire. Local opposition heated up as the Americans prepared to load the obelisk into the *Dessoug*, a converted steamer, for its ocean crossing.

◆ *Had another scuffle with some recalcitrant Arabs today, who tried to scuttle the SS Dessoug, but we routed the rascals before they could do much harm. They ran like jack rabbits the minute we opened fire. What yarns I'll give Luis to spin!*

JOURNAL OF FRANK READE JR.
(APRIL 24, 1880)

They got the obelisk to New York intact, then had to laboriously haul it through the city. Cleopatra's Needle finally reached its destination in Central Park 112 days after landing at Staten Island. Frank Sr. and Henry Gorringe oversaw its installation in January 1881. ☆☆

Emily Reade, 1881.

Frank Sr. removes Cleopatra's Needle from Egypt before transporting it to Central Park in New York.

33

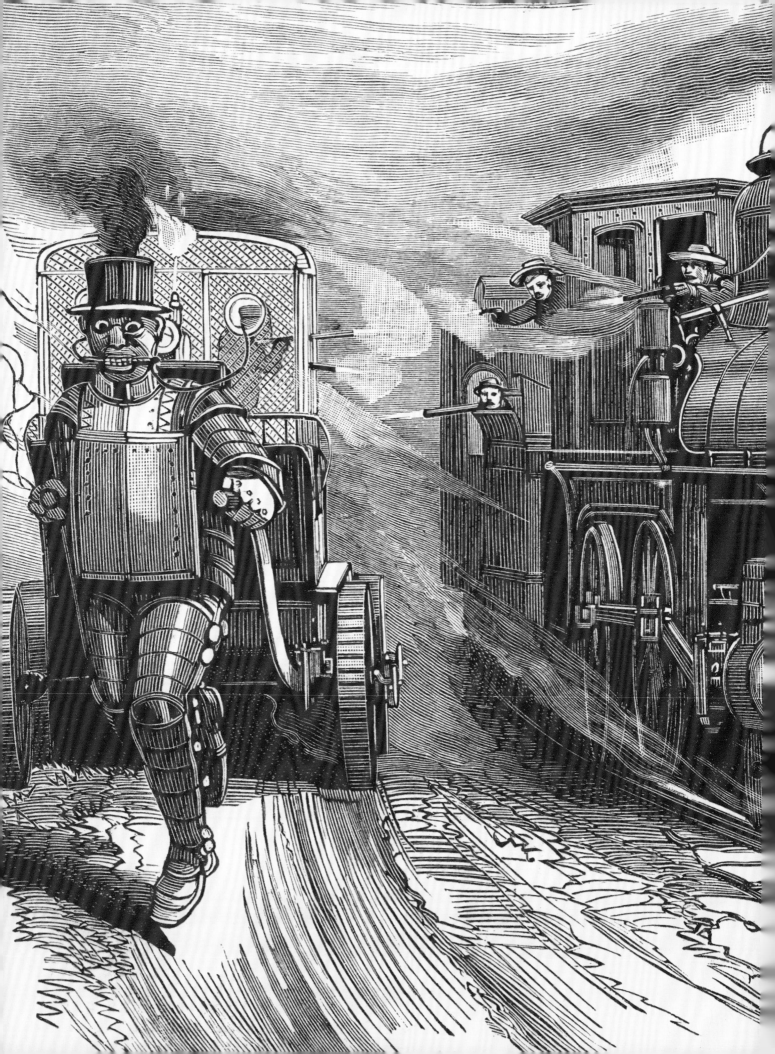

# STEAM
# TEAM

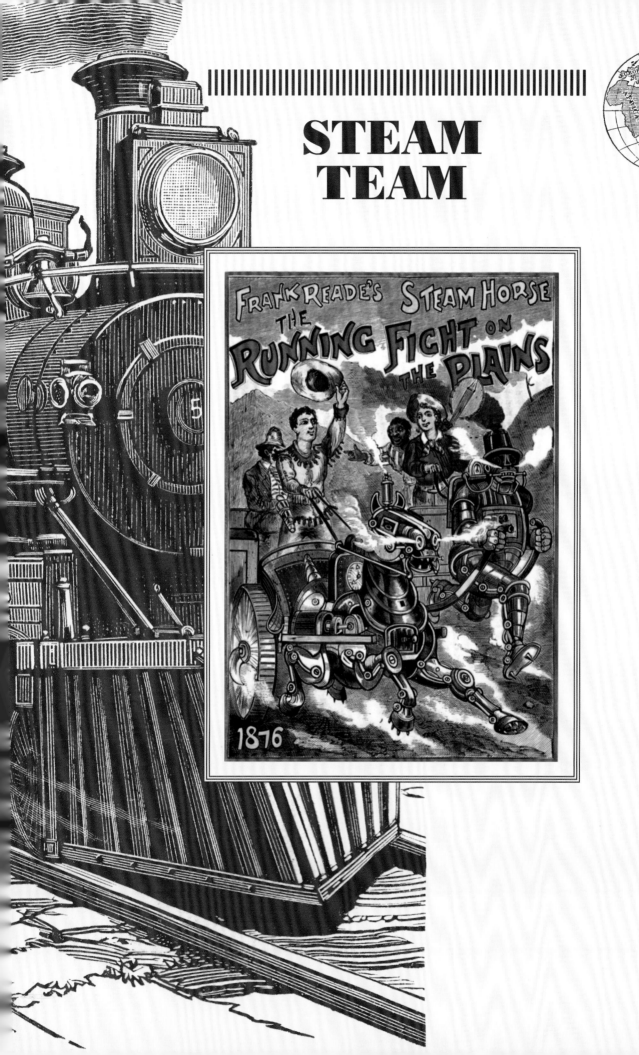

FRANK READE'S STEAM HORSE
THE RUNNING FIGHT ON THE PLAINS

1876

## Frank Reade Jr. AND HIS NEW
# STEAM MAN — or —
## THE YOUNG INVENTOR'S TRIP TO THE FAR EAST
*Frank Reade Library #1*

### CHAPTER I
### *A Great Wager*

Frank Reade was noted the world over as a wonderful and distinguished inventor of marvelous machines in the line of steam and electricity. But he had grown old and unable to knock about the world, as he had been wont once to do.

So it happened that his son, Frank Reade, Jr., succeeded his father as a great inventor, even excelling him in variety and complexity of invention. The great machine shops in Readestown were enlarged by young Frank, and new flying machines, electric wonders, and so forth, were brought into being.

But the elder Frank would maintain that, inasmuch as electricity at the time was an undeveloped factor, his invention of the Steam Man was really the most wonderful of all. "It cannot be improved upon," he declared, positively. "Not if steam is used as a motive power."

Frank, Jr., laughed quietly and patted his father on the back. "Dad," he said, with an affectionate, though bantering air, "what would you think if I should produce a most remarkable improvement upon your Steam Man?"

"You can't do it!" declared the senior Reade.

Frank, Jr., said no more, but smiled in a significant manner. One day later, the doors of the secret draughting-room of design were tightly locked and young Frank came forth only to his meals.

For three months this matter of closed doors continued. In the machine shop department, where the parts of machinery were secretly put together, the ring of hammers might have been heard, and a big sign was upon the door: "No admittance!"

*The Steam Horse was built as a novelty by Frank Sr. for his son.*

### CHAPTER II
### *The New Steam Man*

Frank Reade, Jr., drew a roll of papers from his pocket and spread them upon the table. Upon them were the blue print plans and drawings of the mechanism of the Steam Man.

Frank Reade, Senior, examined them carefully and critically. From one piece to another he went and after some time drew a deep breath saying: "Well, young blood is the best after all. I must say, Frank, that I am beat. There is no doubt but that you have improved upon my Steam Man. I congratulate you."

"Thank you," said Frank Reade, Jr., with gratification.

"But I am anxious to see this marvel at work."

"You shall," replied the young inventor. "To-morrow the Steam Man will go out of the shop upon his trial trip."

A few minutes later Frank Reade, Jr., was on the way to his own house. He was in a particularly happy frame of mind.

The idea of traveling through the wilds of the West was a thrilling one. Frank could already picture the effect of the Steam Man upon the wild savages of the plains and the outlaws of Western Kansas and Colorado. Also the level floor-like prairie of that region would afford excellent traveling for the new invention.

Frank Reade, Jr., was a lover of adventure. It was an inborn love. The prospect before him fired his very soul. It was just what he desired.

The next morning at an early hour, Frank was at the engine house of the steel works. The wide doors were thrown open and a wonderful sight revealed.

There stood the Steam Man. Fire was burning in the furnace inside the iron man, steam was hissing from the retort, and smoke was pouring from the funnel hat.

### Frank Reade Jr. AND HIS
# STEAM HORSE
### *Frank Reade Library #14*

Frank and the Steam Horse flew in a straight line over the plains. Barney and Pomp rode beside him with the Steam Man.

Frank had just decided to put on a full head of steam, when Pomp hailed him with a signal whistle. Frank shut off steam and allowed Barney to drive the man up close to the horse. "What's the matter?" asked Frank.

"Pomp just took a peep with the telescope," said Barney, "and he saw a band of murderous outlaws about four miles ahead. They are the worst on the plains, and I move that we try to clean 'em out alone. What do you say?"

"How many are there?"

"Eight or ten."

"I'll do it," said Frank, diving down into the wonderful trunk, "and here's the article that will do the business." He hauled forth a curious wire work. When stretched out it was about twelve feet long and four or five wide, made of very strong crossed wires, and looking capable of holding considerable weight.

They watched Frank closely while the genius tied the sides of the wire work to the insides of the wagons as they then stood, and made them fast.

"Now drive up close, pull the slack of the wire into your wagon, and then travel. Put on thirty pounds of steam, and we'll run steadily together."

His orders were obeyed, and in two minutes they were rattling across the plains at a smashing pace, close together, and rapidly nearing the band of cutthroats. These latter suddenly spied them, and tried hard to escape in a compact body, and then Frank cried: "Forty pounds of steam! Hurrah!"

And like two immense bolts the Steam Horse and the Steam Man shot down upon the flying band, and as they neared them, Frank cried: "Spread!"

They spread out slightly, rushed on like flashes, and the extended screen of wire pushed the men kiting from the ground and sent them flying. Men went whirling high into the air; and went tumbling over the ground like tops, and all sorts of weapons flew around with the force of the shock, for the solid weight of two immense machines had been sufficient to knock over every living object.

Many were killed instantly; others were left dying on the ground; some few were left to scamper away; but very nearly the entire party of men were stretched out by the one grand rush, and onward dashed the man and horse once more.

And as they rushed onward they caught sight of a single fugitive, who had been cut off from his men and fallen to the ground. Iron spikes crashed through the villain's brain, stretching him dead upon the plain, killed by the wonderful Steam Horse. **FR**

# RETURN
## *to the* LAND *of the*
# PHARAOHS

FRANK JR. AND EMILIE married after he got home. He spent his first year of wedded life in Readestown, building a new electric land vehicle, the *Valiant*—but his heart was still in Egypt. He was getting ready to field-test his new invention when one of his English friends invited him back to Alexandria for a visit in 1882.

Frank Jr. was off like a shot, assuring the pregnant Emilie that he'd be back within a few months. Then a revolution broke out while he was in Egypt, and he stuck around to help the British Royal Navy put it down.

➤ *I could not, of course, bring my dear Emilie to such a dangerous place, not with her being in a family way. This proved to be a wise choice, for Alexandria lies half in ruins now—its European Quarter set afire and plundered by rioting Arabs, the city bombarded by the British fleet. For several hours, the roar of guns and the shrieks of passing shot and shell were the only sounds one could hear.*

*Afterward I took the* Valiant *on patrol to search for survivors, through hot and smoky streets filled with debris from fallen walls and lined with burning buildings. To my surprise, near the Grand Square of Mehmet Ali, in the heart of the city, I encountered a contingent of the American Navy!*

JOURNAL OF FRANK READE JR. (JULY 16, 1882)

Frank Jr. and Emilie are saluted by an honor guard on their wedding day.

A detachment of U.S. Marines, under the command of Lieutenant Littleton Tazewell Waller, had come ashore from the USS *Lancaster*. Their official mission was "to protect American interests during warfare between British and Egyptians and looting of the city of Alexandria by Arabs."

Waller and Frank Jr. would encounter each other again while protecting American interests in the Caribbean years later.

Frank Jr. got home from Egypt three weeks after his son, Frank Reade III, was born. This, too, came as a surprise to Kate, who wrote in her journal, "Papa missed my brother's birth? No wonder they never saw eye to eye." ✫✫

A dime-novel version of the *Valiant* battles "recalcitrant Arabs."

A detachment of U.S. Marines, under the command of Littleton Waller, patrols Alexandria after the ancient Egyptian city is bombarded by the British fleet in 1882.

The *Valiant*
in Egypt,
1882.

# ARABIAN ADVENTURES

Frank Reade Jr.'s
## DESERT EXPLORER
— or —
### THE UNDERGROUND CITY OF THE SAHARA
*Frank Reade Library #80*

**D**own into the depression the *Explorer* ran. There was a mighty cavelike opening in the sand. And into this the machine entered. The next moment, the explorers gave exclamations of wonderment.

They were in a mighty high arched structure, a veritable peristyle at one end, with pillars of the most exquisite architecture. The floor was of finely polished stone, and every indication showed that this had once been the palace of kings.

There was a light of triumph in Frank's eyes. "What did I tell you?" he cried. "Is it not fine?"

"Grand!" exclaimed Prof. Alwise. "Oh, here is full scope for the archæologist!"

The machine rolled slowly on among the mighty pillars and over the stone floor. Frank went into the pilot house with Barney. The search-light was now employed. All dark passages were made light as day, and thus the machine went on.

From one stately paved court to another the machine passed. So high-arched and spacious were the buildings that the *Explorer* could go anywhere. But finally they came to a passage too narrow for it to pass.

Nothing as yet had been seen of the Bedouins.

# THE WHITE DESERT — or —
## Frank Reade Jr.'s TRIP TO THE
## LAND OF TOMBS
### *Frank Reade Library #155*

Jaggs now took his position as the spokesman for Frank, for he knew the Egyptian tongue well. "Who are you?" asked Jaggs.

"I am Mustapha El Hamed, the Secretary General of the Noble Khedive of Egypt," responded the officer grandly. "What do you upon the soil of the followers of Mohammed?"

"We are American travelers," replied Jaggs, "we are permitted by special passports to conduct explorations in the Desert of Mem."

"You obtained your permit under misrepresentation," replied the Secretary General. "You represented yourselves as American scientists, but you have come here to recover the treasures of Shek. All gold found in Egypt belongs to the Khedive, my most noble lord!"

"Not all, but three-fifths, sire!" replied Jaggs, coolly. "You are a little bit hasty. Allow that is our purpose, what do you ask of us?"

"That you deliver yourselves and your air ship up to us. We shall take you before the Khedive for just punishment! As you are foreigners, it is likely that the Khedive will be merciful to you, provided you surrender your air ship to him and leave the country."

Jaggs communicated all this to Frank, who laughed and said: "Tell him that I have no idea of surrendering to him. We will deliver to him the Khedive's three-fifths of the treasure. These are our only terms."

El Hamed was furious when Jaggs made his reply. He raised himself in his saddle and shouted: "Death to the invaders! May the curse of the Prophet rest upon them!" Then the entire Egyptian cavalcade fired a volley at the air ship.

But the bullets did no harm.

Frank was in the pilot house. For a moment he was undecided what move to make. He disliked extremely the idea of slaughtering any of the Arabs. But yet he saw no other way. If they should once enter the temple they would be sure to find the gold, and that they would confiscate all of it there was no doubt.

"Begorra, Mister Frank!" cried Barney; "shall we give it to them back again?"

"Wait a bit," said Frank. But the words had hardly left his lips when the Arabs came forward at full charge. With wild yells and the discharge of fire-arms, they rode down upon the air ship.

Barney and Pomp did not wait for orders, but blazed away. However, their fire was but a drop in the bucket. It did not have any effect upon the foe. Frank saw that if the weight of the cavalcade struck the air ship, some harm might be done.

Quick as a flash he pressed the helice lever, and the air ship rose about twenty feet. The array of charging horsemen thus went under it. Their astonishment and chagrin was great. Like a surging mass of angry fiends, they swirled under the air ship's hull.

Frank saw that the only remedy which could be employed was a drastic one. So he took a dynamite bomb from the locker, and stepped out on deck. He hurled it into the verge of the throng. But as he did so, his foot slipped unwittingly. The bomb did not go as far as he had intended.

In that instant it exploded with terrific force. The effect was most startling. And, in fact, it proved as disastrous to the air ship as to the Arabs.

There was a terrific roar, like a pack of artillery. The air was filled with flame and flying debris. More than one of the great columns of the peristyle was shattered, and a huge fragment was hurled against the air ship's hull. As it struck the *Osiris*, just under the pilot house and by the engine room, our adventurers were all thrown from their feet, and the air ship reeled and swayed.

Then it sank down right among the struggling array of horsemen. Frank pressed the lever to raise the air ship again, and to his horror he found that it would not respond. "My soul!" he gasped; "the machinery is ruined!" **FR**

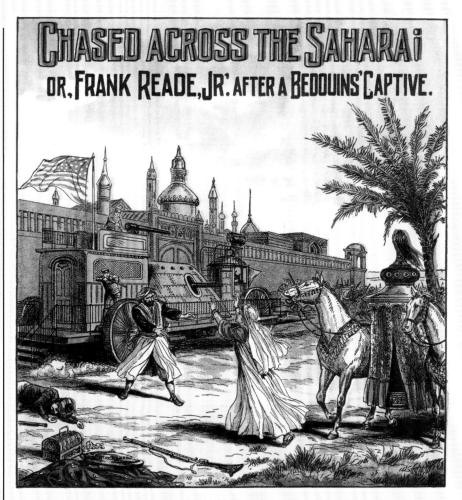

*This story was inspired by rare but real kidnappings of American citizens for ransom. The most famous example was the Perdicaris Incident, which became the basis of a Hollywood movie called* The Wind and the Lion *starring Sean Connery.*

# FRANK READE

## WEEKLY MAGAZINE,

### Containing Stories of Adventures on Land, Sea & in the Air.

*Issued Weekly—By Subscription $2.50 per year. Entered as Second Class Matter at the New York Post Office, 1902, by Frank Tousey.*

No. 6.     NEW YORK, DECEMBER 5, 1902.     Price 5 Cents.

Frank sent the blinding rays of the searchlight down and transfigured the whole scene. **Crack!** Mardo Turgi, with the order for Pomp's execution upon his lips, threw up his arms, and fell  It was just in the nick of time.

# 2
# AGE *of*
# ELECTRICITY

AT ONLY TWENTY-ONE YEARS OLD, Frank Reade Jr. was already an accomplished scientist, world traveler, combat veteran, and father. Ever restless, he still felt driven to create something of his own, something new. In the 1880s, as inventors around the world raced to crack the secrets of the horseless carriage, submarines, and powered flight, Frank Jr. beat them all to it. He used electricity to conquer land, sea, and air.

During the late eighteenth century, steam cars built by wealthy enthusiasts began to appear on roads. In 1833, Walter Hancock's *Enterprise* was the first of several steam buses that provided regular commuter service. Because steam engines were already an established technology, Frank Jr. focused his research on electric-powered vehicles.

## The END of STEAM

STEAM-POWERED vehicles were old hat by this time. Recognizing that electricity would drive the world of tomorrow, Frank Jr. ardently pursued his research into electric power sources, motors, and storage and transmission systems.

➤ *Frank entered into an animated description of the electric machinery that gave so much power for so little weight. "It is the motive power of the future," he said. "Steam will give way to it, and thus . . . the world will become completely revolutionized."*

"FRANK READE, JR., EXPLORING MEXICO IN HIS NEW AIR-SHIP," *FRANK READE LIBRARY* #35

Over the course of his life, Frank Jr. would build hundreds of experimental vehicles and travel the globe. He learned something new from each one—starting with his first electric land rover, the *Valiant,* which had served him so well in Egypt that he decided to take it to Texas. ✩✩

Frank Reade Jr. in his wetsuit.

# THE VALIANT

Frank Jr. dispatches outlaws with an electrified wire connected to a dime-novel depiction of the *Valiant*.

**F**RANK READE JR. loved tinkering with engines and vehicles because they moved and changed—they could do different things and take you to different places. As Kate Reade put it in her journal, "Papa was always voyaging, never arriving."

The *Valiant*, his first all-terrain land rover, was the first practical electric land vehicle, predating the work of electric car pioneers Gustave Trouvé and Thomas Parker. Built as a war chariot, it sported intimidating features such as twenty-inch scythes mounted on the hubcaps, which could be removed when traveling in close quarters. The six-foot spike on its nose, akin to a naval ram, was a design element seen on many of Frank

The *Valiant* runs down a bison in another fictional version of the electric rover.

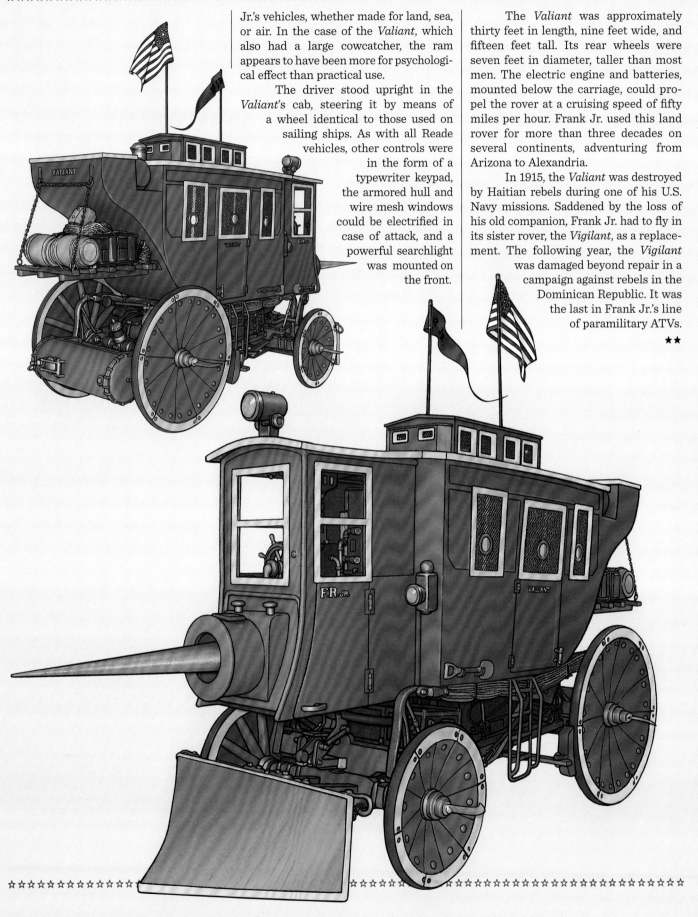

Jr.'s vehicles, whether made for land, sea, or air. In the case of the *Valiant*, which also had a large cowcatcher, the ram appears to have been more for psychological effect than practical use.

The driver stood upright in the *Valiant*'s cab, steering it by means of a wheel identical to those used on sailing ships. As with all Reade vehicles, other controls were in the form of a typewriter keypad, the armored hull and wire mesh windows could be electrified in case of attack, and a powerful searchlight was mounted on the front.

The *Valiant* was approximately thirty feet in length, nine feet wide, and fifteen feet tall. Its rear wheels were seven feet in diameter, taller than most men. The electric engine and batteries, mounted below the carriage, could propel the rover at a cruising speed of fifty miles per hour. Frank Jr. used this land rover for more than three decades on several continents, adventuring from Arizona to Alexandria.

In 1915, the *Valiant* was destroyed by Haitian rebels during one of his U.S. Navy missions. Saddened by the loss of his old companion, Frank Jr. had to fly in its sister rover, the *Vigilant*, as a replacement. The following year, the *Vigilant* was damaged beyond repair in a campaign against rebels in the Dominican Republic. It was the last in Frank Jr.'s line of paramilitary ATVs. ★★

The *Valiant* weaves its way through a small group of bison, once the most numerous large mammal on the planet. With the coming of Europeans in North America, bison herds that formerly stretched to the horizon and numbered in the millions were decimated by hunters. Only a few hundred bison were left in the United States by the mid-1880s.

# GERONIMO!

**A**S A YOUNG MAN, Frank Reade Jr. couldn't stay away from Indian Territory and the Wild West. Kate Reade, in her journal, speculated that "maybe Papa gravitated to the Southern Plains because they looked like another planet. They sure looked nothing like Delaware." She would learn the real reasons eventually, but not yet.

In 1883, the U.S. Army mounted an expedition to track and capture the warrior known to white men as Geronimo. One of the toughest Apache leaders, Geronimo fiercely resisted the inexorable constriction of his people. He repeatedly escaped from reservations, eluding U.S. and Mexican government forces for years at a time.

When reports reached Readestown that a young boy named Charlie McComas had been orphaned and kidnapped by renegade Apache, Frank Jr. seemed to take it personally. He headed west with the *Valiant* and his latest invention, an electric cannon.

➤ *These savages shall not be allowed to persist in defying the law of the United States and committing depredations on innocent folk. I go to aid Gen. Crook, who is preparing a campaign to hunt down the fugitives. Never again will these Apache steal away a young boy from his rightful home.*

JOURNAL OF FRANK READE JR. (APRIL 7, 1883)

## — LOST IN THE SIERRA MADRE —

**G**ENERAL GEORGE CROOK was an experienced Indian fighter who had proven adept at using native scouts and methods to help subdue various tribes. Frank Jr. and Crook's forces, which included 193 Apache scouts, spent months chasing Geronimo's band.

The Apache hid out—and were especially hard to track—in the unforgiving Sierra Madre mountains, which cross the Sonora-Arizona border. It was here that Frank Jr. discovered a critical drawback to his first land vehicle.

➤ *Heat, barrenness, jagged mountain cliffs, steep walled canyons, scant water, or the utter absence of it, these multiplied a hundred fold the prowess of the wily Apaches who had been accustomed for generations to defy these obstacles, to sustain life under these hard conditions. Science itself is defeated here, for Mr. Reade's otherwise formidable electric battle carriage could not follow us down those canyons so dark they seemed bottomless.*

MAJOR G. W. BAIRD, "THE CAPTURE OF GERONIMO'S APACHES," *THE CENTURY,* VOL. 42, NO. 3 (JULY 1891)

## —UNTIL NEXT TIME —

**A**LTHOUGH the *Valiant* couldn't traverse the rugged Sierra Madre, Frank Jr.'s electric gun did prove decisive in rounding up many of the fugitives. He helped Crook bring in three hundred Apache by June. Geronimo was not among them.

Native Americans on reservations were often at the mercy of corrupt agents in the Office of Indian Affairs, who misappropriated money designated for the welfare of the tribes. Abuse of power and poor conditions on "the rez" prompted more than one uprising.

THE REASON OF THE INDIAN OUTBREAK.
General Miles declares that the Indians are starved into rebellion.

Geronimo resisted U.S. Army control for years. Frank Jr. pursued the elusive Apache military leader on two separate occasions, through craggy terrain that motivated the inventor to develop his first airship.

➤ *The cannon functions exactly according to design, firing bolts of lightning that send up great showers of earth and rock. Often this alone terrorizes the savages into submission, with no need for loss of life. Being connected to the* Valiant's *dynamos, however, the gun is not useful until the Apache has emerged from his mountainous lair.*

JOURNAL OF FRANK READE JR. (JUNE 3, 1883)

A dime-novel interpretation of Frank Jr.'s *Valiant,* this time dubbed the *Warrior.*

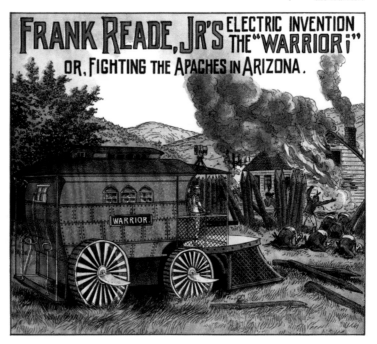

The *Valiant* in the American West, 1883.

Frank Jr. was mortified by what he saw as the failure of his marvelous electric vehicle. Determined to conquer failure, he headed back to Readestown with Pomp and Barney. "Chasing Injuns" would have to wait while he invented a better solution.

◆ *Mister Frank was in a fair rage and fixing to smash up the Valiant's instruments! I went running to the pilot-house soon as I heard Pomp's call. The both of us had to wrestle the man down and sit on him till he came to his senses. He's been working away on his flying machine drawings ever since, while Pompei steers us homeward in the Valiant.*

BARNEY O'SHEA, LETTER TO BETTY O'SHEA
(JULY 1, 1883)

Geronimo surrendered to General Crook early in 1884, but that wasn't the end of the Apache warrior's resistance. Frank Jr. would soon have another chance at capturing him. Next time, the young inventor planned to have the upper hand.  ✫✫

The *Valiant* stops in Wichita to pick up supplies.

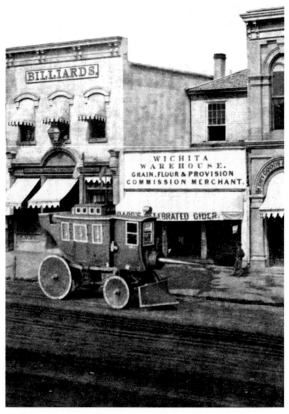

# READE
# LANDSHIPS

*The* Thunderer *was the largest vehicle Readeworks ever produced. Before the advent of linked caterpillar tracks like the ones used on tanks today, behemoths such as the* Thunderer *tended to get stuck in soft ground, sand, and mud.*

Frank Reade Jr.'s
NEW ELECTRIC TERROR
## THE THUNDERER
— or — THE SEARCH FOR THE
## TARTAR'S CAPTIVE
*Frank Reade Library #25*

### CHAPTER II
### *On the Steppes*

The *Thunderer* was, as Frank had said, truly an ominous machine. The body was cigar shaped, with keen rams at either end. It was of lightest steel, rolled fine and hard, and while not impervious to a cannon ball would easily withstand bullets.

There were seven circular bull's-eye windows in the hull. At either end there was a porthole, through which projected the barrel of a pneumatic dynamite gun, a wonderful invention of Frank's.

The body of the *Thunderer* rested upon cleverly constructed framework, with two reversible circles for the proper turning of the machine in any direction desired. Eight wheels with broad-grooved tires with axles driven by electric shafts connected with the electrical machinery inside the hull. By this arrangement the *Thunderer* could be made to go in any direction desired.

Upon the top of the hull was a square frame, with thin network of finest steel to cover it. This made a sort of

*Sparks shoot out from the undercarriage of the* Electric Turret, *startling horses as it crosses the Great Plains.*

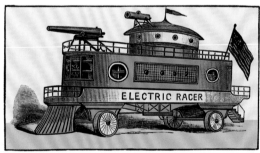

deck upon which the voyagers could sit and view the country about. There were loopholes in this netting to fire through in case of an attack. Above the network was the tower or pilot-house, and on the top of that was a powerful electric search-light.

Frank now took his visitor on board the *Thunderer*. The pilot house was in itself a region of wonder. There was the key board, with its multitudinous connections, and by means of which the ship was controlled and regulated.

The hull was divided into three compartments. The one in the center, and connected by stairway with the pilot tower, was the dynamo and engine room with the wonderful electric storage system, which was Frank Reade, Jr.'s secret.

Forward was a delightful parlor, fitted up luxuriously with rich furniture, a small library, valuable charts, instruments and curios. Aft, or properly at the other end of the *Thunderer*, was the sleeping rooms and bunks. There was also a galley, and dining area with the choicest silver and china.

The young American was delighted. He could hardly contain himself. "It will be simply grand traveling across the steppes in this way!" he declared. "And we shall certainly succeed in defeating Mardo Turgi and rescuing Madge!"

Frank Reade, Jr.'s intention to visit Tartary with the *Thunderer* leaked out in some way that evening, and before morning the news had been telegraphed to every city in the United States.

A tremendous sensation was created, especially in official circles at Washington. By order of the President, assurances were sent to Frank that he would travel through Asia under the protection of the United States Government and with the Executive sanction. Everywhere, the excitement was most intense as the romantic nature of Frank's errand was made known.

## CHAPTER XII
### *Exciting Work*

The *Thunderer* glided into the ravine and began to make its way upward. In less than twenty minutes the machine was upon the plateau. Frank sent it forward noiselessly and shadow-like to a point upon an eminence from whence they could look down into the stronghold. The whole interior of the fortress yard was visible. And a thrilling scene was witnessed.

It was just at the moment when Pomp was led forth to be executed by the vengeful Mardo Turgi. The brutal Tartar executioners had just advanced with their gleaming swords and stood over the condemned darky.

A great cry went up from all on board the *Thunderer*.

"My God, what is that?"

"Some one is going to be slaughtered!"

"Heavens, it is Pomp!"

"Save him!"

Barney was the first one to act. The Celt saw the awful deadly peril of his confrere the first of all. His blood was at boiling pitch. "Whurro!" he yelled, "they shall never kill the likes of him!" Quick as a flash he raised his rifle and took aim.

At the same moment Frank sent the blinding rays of the search-lights down and transfigured the whole scene.

Crack! Mardo Turgi, with the order for Pomp's execution upon his lips, threw up his arms and fell. It was just in the nick of time. The order to cut Pomp's head off was never uttered.

Crack! Crack! The two executioners dropped.

Pomp in an instant saw the search-light's glare, and knew what it meant. He acted quickly. With wonderful presence of mind he seized the sword from the hands of one of the dead executioners. He began to lay about him furiously.

At that moment Frank Reade, Jr., pulled the valve of the electric gun. A projectile struck the fort wall. There was a roaring explosion, and the air was full of flying debris. When it cleared away it was seen that a huge hole had been blown in the wall of the fort.

It was a breach full ten feet wide. Down through it went the *Thunderer* full tilt and head on. **FR**

# WHIRLYBIRD

Fueled by a reservoir of buried fury over his inability to capture Geronimo using the *Valiant*, Frank Jr. attacked his work in Reades-town with a newfound resolve to unlock the secrets of flight. Instead of an airplane or a dirigible, though, he aimed to build a fast, highly maneuverable helicopter airship. It was an impossible feat, given the technology of the day.

Undaunted, Frank Jr. threw himself into inventing a new kind of rotor blade and electric motor. He didn't know it at the time, but his electrical research paralleled work being done in Paris by Nikola Tesla, the father of alternating current electricity.

Frank Jr. started by testing his designs in a one-man craft. In December 1883, he achieved the impossible. He lifted off in the world's first helicopter, piloting it in a circle around Reade-works, one hundred feet above the ground.

◆ *The rotascope is a great success. My trajectory was fully controlled with such ease that I could spare one hand from the instruments, so as to wave a greeting at the astonished upturned faces beneath me. Now to apply the same principles to a larger vessel, one capable of transporting a crew and cargo.*

Journal of Frank Reade Jr. (December 22, 1883)

Frank Jr. with an early prototype of his helicopter rotor shaft and motor.

## — UP, UP, AND AWAY —

Frank Sr., impressed by his son's designs and dedication, put the young man in charge of Readeworks' new Electrical Division. The company had grown large enough to employ a small army of men.

An army was about what it took to ramp up production of Frank Jr.'s ambitious new project: a gigantic electric airship with multiple rotors, a majestic armored hull, and electric cannon. In only six months, Readeworks produced the *Zephyr,* a unique helicopter airship destined to be the first of many. Frank Jr. and Emilie's second child, Kate, was born during this same period.

Frank Jr. tests his first helicopter on the streets of Readestown, 1883.

A helicopter rotor shaft being manufactured at the Readeworks foundry.

◆ *You should see the marvels Frank is building! Yesterday he took me on the first flight of his air-ship, after persistent persuasion. For many miles we sailed in the air above the Delaware River, its mighty waters and lush valley rolling far below us. It felt as if we were carried along by the hand of God Himself. I must ask Frank to take me aloft after dark, that I may use my telescope to observe the stars from this new vantage.*

EMILIE READE, LETTER TO SARAH FRANCES WHITING
(JUNE 30, 1884)

Frank Jr. was so proud of his accomplishments that he decided to keep them to himself. He didn't mind spreading general information, or misinformation, about his technology. But he always strove to keep the technical details out of the public record. No one would ever be able to read about his discoveries, let alone buy them, as his father had done with Zadoc Dederick's Steam Man patent.

Chartroom of the airship *White Cruiser.* The spittoon was for Barney's use. Interior photos of Readeworks craft were allowed, so long as they didn't show any technological secrets.

Parlor room of the *White Cruiser.* Frank Reade Jr.'s youthful enjoyment of "high-class grub and furnishings" found its expression in the living spaces aboard his vehicles, which are lavishly described in many *Frank Reade* dime novels.

An accurate depiction of the *Flying Scud* under construction at Readeworks, from *Harper's Weekly* magazine (at left), compared to the same subject as depicted by *Frank Reade Library* (below). At Frank Reade Jr.'s direction, Readeworks vehicles (especially helicopters) were depicted inaccurately in dime novels so that the technology would be harder to copy.

❧ *Where so many other men have failed, I have succeeded in achieving powered flight. The secret is mine alone; I'll not share it with lesser minds by filing patent applications. I will use my inventions exclusively for the benefit of myself and my family, my business, and my country.*

JOURNAL OF FRANK READE JR. (JUNE 29, 1884)

✪ ✪

Jack Wright and other Readeworks employees give scale to one of Frank Jr.'s helicopter rotor blades. A standard airplane propeller is also displayed for comparison. This rare photo was found among Frank Jr.'s papers after his death.

# HELICOPTERS

**H**ELICOPTERS have been around in some form for ages. In ancient China, people played with tops made of twisted feathers attached to the end of a bamboo stick. By twirling the stick between their hands, they could generate lift and release the top into free flight, then watch it sail through the air.

Aeronautics expert David Hahn extrapolates the design of a Readeworks helicopter's rotor assembly.

The earliest recorded design of a manned helicopter dates back to 1483, when Leonardo da Vinci conceived of a vertical-lift vehicle with a helical rotor, but he only made models of his design. Gustave de Ponton d'Amécourt demonstrated one of his model *hélicoptères* at the 1868 London Aeronautical Exposition. George Cayley built a working twin-rotor helicopter model in 1792, powered by clock springs.

Many other inventors created powered models during the nineteenth century—but not a full-scale version capable of carrying a man into the sky. Frank Reade Jr. designed and flew the first true helicopter in 1883, at the age of twenty-one, using a lightweight electric engine and revolutionary new rotors.

Newspaper publisher James Gordon Bennett, who financed African exploration by Henry Morton Stanley and sponsored air and sea races, was especially interested in Frank Jr.'s accomplishment. Bennett approached him with a proposal for commercially exploiting the invention, but Frank Jr. turned it down.

Bennett then gave Thomas Edison $1,000 to begin work on a helicopter. Edison failed to produce a practical vehicle, though he did produce an impressive explosion in his lab when one of his models blew up.

Frank Jr.'s secrecy, and his refusal to file patent applications or sell his technology, prevented anyone outside Readeworks from exploiting his breakthroughs. No one else would develop workable vertical takeoff and landing (VTOL) aircraft until the 1920s. Frank Jr. was ahead of even the brilliant Nikola Tesla, who patented a design for a one-man VTOL rotor aircraft called "Apparatus for Aerial Transportation" in 1928.

Eventually, Frank Jr. passed the baton to his daughter, Kate Reade, whose work for the U.S. Navy in the 1930s helped make helicopters practical and birthed an industry of VTOL rotorcraft. ★★

# READE
# AIRSHIPS

*Barney, Frank Jr., and Pomp welcome Frank Sr.'s arrival in the* Catamaran.
*The pontoon-style hull is unusual. Only a few other Readeworks airships used similar designs,
including Frank Jr.'s* Eagle *and, many years later, Kate's* Helios.

### Frank Reade Jr. AND HIS
## QUEEN CLIPPER
#### OF THE CLOUDS (PART 1)
*Frank Reade Library* #44

There was something exalting in the sentiments and sensations which the captain and crew of the *Queen Clipper of the Clouds* experienced as the majestic air-ship bore them onward high above the realms of mortals.

The pathless sea of the atmosphere all around them, with its vast infinitude of space—endless and immeasurable—contributed a sense of the grandeur of the unknown universe surrounding our world that caused all to think how little, how insignificant, indeed, was man and all his works.

The grand mechanism of the master power that held all the planets in their orbits and guided their eternal revolutions through the endless cycles of time was out of sight—unseen even as the mighty power that governs the coming and going of the unceasing round of the seasons—yet the air voyagers felt that hidden influence as in a way that caused them to remain awed and silent while all the wondrous panorama of our world was spread out before them like some grand landscape under the wand of a mighty magician.

As the *Queen Clipper of the Clouds* sailed onward, the view from the deck was constantly changing. The scenes blended into each other with all the rare harmony of light, color, and diversity of subject which nature's lavish brush had painted.

There were busy, thriving, western towns; peaceful, sleepy hamlets, where one might think to find at last the new Arcadia; far-reaching farm-lands, yielding bountiful harvests; and vast plains and forests, with streams and rivers threading their verdant depths like threads of silver amidst emerald settings.

And then the sense of infinite solitude and infinite silence, broken only by the unceasing whirr of the helices revolving at the mast-heads, and the slower and more labored beating of the great bow and stern propellers.

The voyagers had indeed entered upon a new world—the world of the atmosphere, and it was an experience tending to expand their minds and render them humble in the sight of the creator of it all.

*Frank Jr., Pompei, Barney, Professor Vaneyke, and Frank Sr. escape the destruction of the airship Flight.*
*So many vehicles were irreparably damaged in the course of their adventures that Pomp remarked in*
*Frank Reade Library #67, "It's the strangest thing that most everything you invent done get broke somehow."*

# FRANK READE

## WEEKLY MAGAZINE,

### Containing Stories of Adventures on Land, Sea & in the Air.

Issued Weekly—By Subscription $2.50 per year.   Application made for Second-Class Entry at N. Y. Post-Office.

No. 43.        NEW YORK, AUGUST 21, 1903.        Price 5 Cents.

# AROUND THE ARCTIC CIRCLE¡

## OR FRANK READE, JR.'S FAMOUS FLIGHT WITH HIS AIR SHIP.

### By "NONAME."

"If we can keep them at bay," declared Frank, "Barney and Pomp will soon come to our rescue."
"We'll do that!" cried Vance. The three men, behind a pile of bowlders, kept
up a fire at the Tartars. This had its effect.

## ON THE GREAT MERIDIAN
### WITH Frank Reade Jr., IN HIS NEW
## AIR-SHIP
— or —
### A TWENTY-FIVE THOUSAND MILE TRIP IN MID-AIR
*Frank Reade Library #119*

If I were to betray my secret," Frank said, "it would revolutionize the world. Our whole political and social life would undergo a change."

"How do you make that out?" asked a friend.

"If people could travel in air-ships safely they could very quickly cross the country, and railway trains and steamboats and other modes of travel would become a thing of the past. The effect upon society could then very readily be seen. It would demand different manners and customs, different styles of living, a revolution in business, and a complete change in our whole social and economic system."

"Then you do not intend to give your discovery to the world?"

"No, sir." The answer was emphatic.

"Why not?" asked the friend in surprise. "What could be the harm?"

"It would be incalculable. For instance, suppose that the French government obtained first the secret of the air-ship from me? She would of course instantly proceed to pay back her score against Germany. Revenge is sweet. By means of the air-ship she could sail over the Kaiser's dominions and raze every city with dynamite. That would involve Europe and perhaps the whole world in war."

The friend was bound to acknowledge the logic of Frank's theory.

"Consequently," continued the young inventor, "I shall prefer to keep my secret to myself." **FR**

Professor Archibald Campion is the father of modern robotics. At the 1893 World's Columbian Exposition in Chicago, he unveiled a prototype mechanical soldier (later nicknamed Boilerplate) for "preventing the deaths of men in the conflicts of nations." Frank Reade Jr., whose robotics research had hit a dead end, would regret turning down Archie's earlier offer of collaboration.

# MEETING
## *of the* MINDS

ASIDE FROM POMP AND BARNEY, Frank Jr.'s best friend was fellow inventor Archibald Campion, who created the marvelous mechanical man known as Boilerplate. They met in 1885, when Archie traveled from Chicago to Readestown to find out if the rumors about Frank Jr. building an electrically powered robot were true.

They were. Now that Frank Jr. had mastered flight, he was taking another crack at inventing an automaton that could walk on its own. By the time Archie visited, Frank Jr. had built a functional Electric Man, but he was still having trouble with the walking.

➤ *Readeworks is all that I had imagined it to be, and more. I suspect you would be enraptured by its enormous machineworks and laboratories, which hold every type of implement and device that could conceivably be useful in work such as ours.*

*As for Reade, I find him difficult to fathom. Clearly he is eager to demonstrate his Electric Man and discuss general principles, but he is uninterested in collaborating with intellectual equals other than his father. I have ascertained that his Electric Man is not capable of true*

*bipedal locomotion and thus would not serve to help advance my own research.*

*What is your opinion of that Tesla fellow, the Serb? I am intrigued by reports about his experiments in Paris and understand he is now in New York working for Edison.*

ARCHIBALD CAMPION, LETTER TO EDWARD FULLERTON (AUGUST 18, 1885)

Although they were both brilliant inventors, in many ways Campion and Reade couldn't have been more different from each other. Based on their first encounter, no one would've predicted that they would develop an enduring comradeship. Frank Jr.'s account of their initial meeting is terse and, as Kate later observed, misunderstands Archie's purpose.

➤ *I had a visit from Archibald Campion, whose patents have been so useful in informing my electrical designs. Precisely the reason I choose not to patent my own inventions. He wanted to join forces with me, but I'll be damned if I'll give him the chance to profit from my ingenuity.*

JOURNAL OF FRANK READE JR. (AUGUST 18, 1885)

➤ *Papa was a rotten judge of character. He thought everyone was out to steal his ideas, even solid old Archie Campion, of all people! It was our good luck that Archie didn't hold it against him.*

KATE READE, LETTER TO ALICE ROOSEVELT (MAY 5, 1933)

☆☆

One of several machine shops in the Readeworks complex.

# READEWORKS

I N **1866,** Frank Sr. selected as the site of Readeworks a remote location north of Philadelphia, on an eastern tributary of the Delaware River. It would enable seagoing vessels to navigate from his planned factory down to the Atlantic Ocean. The Reades gradually acquired surrounding parcels of land, expanding their tract to more than a thousand acres.

By the end of the century, the main factory buildings were the size of football fields. The largest of them produced airships, while the others manufactured land and sea vehicles, all for the Reades' own use. Among the collection of struc-

tures was an Electrical Building that developed engines for the Reade vehicles, as well as standard dynamos and batteries for commercial sale; a Mechanical Building, which housed what today would be called a robotics division; and a Weapons Building, where Frank Jr.'s pneumatic guns and electric cannon were created.

The growing labor force required by Readeworks spurred the development of Readestown. It was a company town, but only in the sense that the Reades owned most of the real estate and the electric utility. The water and gas companies, grocers and other local businesses,

A wheelhouse for one of Frank Jr.'s airships under construction at Readeworks.

An 1890 photo of the inventive team at Readeworks. Left to right: Frank Reade Sr., at this time primarily an engineering consultant on large-scale public projects; Electric Bob, whose task of keeping the numerous electrical vehicles operational was Herculean; Frank Reade Jr., who worked employees hard but paid them well; and Jack Wright, who helped turn Frank Jr.'s mechanical drawings into reality.

and the hospital were all independently owned, and workers were paid in U.S. dollars, not in company scrip.

In fact, Frank Jr.'s secretiveness about his proprietary technology literally paid off for his employees. To reduce their incentive to sell information about Readeworks, Frank Jr. compensated his people well and rewarded loyalty with handsome pensions. He also limited workers' access to valuable information, compartmentalizing the production process so that no one except himself and his foremen, Jack Wright and Electric Bob, ever had all the information needed to assemble an entire device. Finally, Frank Jr. succeeded in creating a cult of personality, based on his dime-novel persona, that commanded loyalty from many employees.

Frank Jr.'s treatment of his workers was extraordinary in an era when people were fighting and dying for an eight-hour workday and a living wage. In addition to sending armed forces against strikers, many businessmen leveraged their influence in politics and media to wage a propaganda war. Workers protesting for safe working conditions were branded as "anarchists," and newspaper editorials issued dire warnings that banning child labor would hurt the economy. By contrast, Frank Jr., although a demanding boss, was well respected, and his nickname "Junior" was used affectionately at Readeworks. ★★

An 1882 engraving of a solar collector on the grounds of Readeworks. Augustin Mouchot developed the technology, publicly demonstrating it in 1878. The Reades adapted his design and utilized it at their factory, but it wasn't efficient enough to power their vehicles.

Postcard of Readeworks in the 1880s. Visible in this photo are the airship *Sky Pilot*, at the factory's mooring tower, and the gunship *Centennial*, docked in front of the main entrance. In the left background is a railroad line that transported supplies to and from Readeworks. In the foreground is the ATV *Valiant* parked in front of a cottage called The Shed, which housed a small reference library. Here the Reades occasionally retreated from the factory for quiet study.

Frank Jr. holds baby Kate Reade in the conning tower of the *Brizo* outside Readeworks. With them are Frank Sr. and Jack Wright.

Pompei shows off the latest submersible at the Readeworks launching dock.

Readeworks employees, friends, and Pennsylvania dignitaries witness the launch of Frank Jr.'s latest sub.

☆☆☆☆☆☆☆☆☆☆☆☆☆☆☆☆☆☆☆☆☆☆☆☆☆☆☆☆☆☆☆☆☆☆☆☆☆☆☆☆☆☆☆☆☆☆☆☆☆☆☆☆☆☆☆☆☆☆☆☆

Frank Jr. demonstrates his new airship while Frank Sr. leans on the table in the Model Room at Readeworks. Every Reade vehicle began its development as a model before a full-scale version was made.

Frank Jr. and Pompei with the Electric Man in the Australian outback, 1885.

# *The* ELECTRIC MAN

**F**rank Jr.'s new automaton, the Electric Man, was a big improvement over the Steam Men because it didn't need to constantly burn coal or haul around a fuel supply. Powered by the same dual-battery technology Frank Jr. developed for his electric vehicles, the Electric Man could travel virtually forever without stopping.

Frank Jr. decided to test it out by prospecting in the vast, sparsely populated Australian outback, where there was mineral wealth galore— diamonds, gold, silver, copper, uranium, and more—but no mining industry yet.

*◆ The Electric Man performs very capably as transport. We have encountered several kangaroos, whose enormous hind legs can propel them along at forty miles per hour, and the Electric Man has outsped them every time. It is an unfortunate fact, however, that the man cannot be detached from the cart and thus cannot serve as a miner.*

FRANK READE JR., LETTER TO JACK WRIGHT
(NOVEMBER 23, 1885)

Strong though it was, the Electric Man couldn't do any digging. Like its predecessors, the Steam Men, it wasn't designed to operate independently of the vehicle it pulled. So Frank Jr. relied on his trusty cohorts, Pompei and Barney, to help turn a profit.

◆ *You wouldn't believe what riches we're finding—diamonds and gold what no-one's ever touched! It's a hard day's work me and Pomp are up to, and Mister Frank don't trust no-one else to be doing it. But we get to keep a percentage like usual, so you can expect that a certain pretty little missus will be receiving some fine gifts upon my return.*

BARNEY O'SHEA, LETTER TO BETTY O'SHEA
(NOVEMBER 26, 1885)

Frank Jr.'s account of the mining expedition gave Kate new insight into the finances behind Readeworks, something she had always wondered about.

◆ *So that's how Papa could afford to keep churning out his airships and other contraptions without ever selling them. He was a treasure hunter, just like in the stories! The crafty old devil. I knew Grandfather's commissions and Papa's government contracts couldn't have paid for it all.*

JOURNAL OF KATE READE (MAY 14, 1934)
☆☆

THE
Electric Man
OF
Frank Reade
IN AUSTRALIA.

# ELECTRIC ADVENTURES

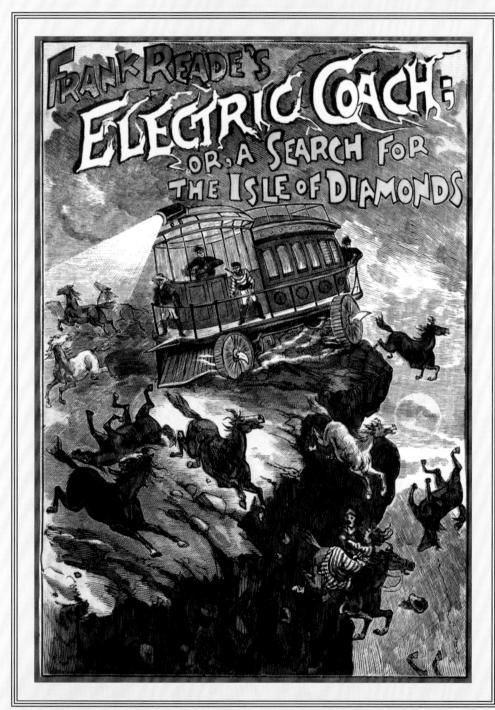

*Although electric cars enjoyed a brief popularity spike at the turn of the twentieth century, corporate petroleum interests ensured that the combustion engine would dominate the market. Today, most of the world relies on a century-old technology to power vehicles because of the profits and clout generated by oil.*

THE
**ELECTRIC HORSE**
— or —
Frank Reade Jr. and His Father
IN SEARCH OF THE
**LOST TREASURE**
OF THE **PERUVIANS**
*Frank Reade Library #38*

### CHAPTER I
### *Frank and His Father*

**J**ust about a year ago Frank Reade, Jr., returned from Australia, after making his successful trip through that country with the Electric Man.

When Frank reached home he found his father hard at work on a new invention, with which the old gentleman meant to surprise his son. He tried to keep it a secret from Frank, Jr., but the latter's curiosity was excited and he found out what his father was up to.

Then the two put their heads together and the result was the Electric Horse, after months of study and diligent experiment and labor. The great inventor and scientist and his son were well satisfied with the outcome of their efforts.

### CHAPTER XXIII
### *Frank, Jr., Experiments with His Electric Gauntlets*

**W**hile Barney slipped on the suit of chain mail, Frank produced a pair of steel-plated gauntlet gloves. On his back he strapped

*Barney operates equipment in the wagon, Frank Jr. stands on the upper deck, Pompei takes the reins, and Frank Sr. explains the workings of their Electric Horse to former president Rutherford B. Hayes.*

a small knapsack and then drew on the steel gloves and connected them with the knapsack by means of flexible wires, jointed every few inches and insulated by rubber tubes, which ran over his shoulders and down his arms.

These preparations were completed in a moment, and then Frank and Barney seized their arms and slipped out of the carriage.

As Frank and Barney suddenly appeared before the surprised natives, the sunlight illuminated their polished suits of mail, and reflected a thousand brilliant lights, making the men in armor look as though they were incased in suits of flame. Like supernatural beings they seemed to the Ticunas priests, who fell back for a moment in awe, and stricken with superstitious fears.

Every time Frank, Jr., seized a native, the electric gloves gave him a powerful shock, something like a stroke of lightning, though not so severe of course. Frank keeled the natives over in every direction.

When the reinforcements came up, led by a giant chief, Frank, Jr., advanced toward him, holding out his hand. Hand-shaking is a custom among the Ticunas, and the big chief thought Frank wanted to make friends, seeing he was in a tight place. The crafty native counted on seizing his extended hand in seeming friendship, with a grip of iron, to jerk the young inventor off his feet, and thus make him a prisoner.

In a moment the young genius grasped the hand of the Herculean chief in his steel gauntlet. Then, with a yell of pain, the huge fellow sprang up, as though hurled into the air by some invisible power, and fell in a heap, shocked into insensibility.

Frank leaped over the fallen Ticunas, and dashed among his followers, shocking them right and left with every touch of the magical gloves.

Meanwhile, through a telescope, Mr. Reade, Sr., had witnessed the conflict in progress at the scaffold-tombs, and becoming alarmed when he saw the reinforcements coming from the Indian village, he hastened to get the Electric Horse and carriage in motion, and directed its course straight toward the scaffolds.

But when the Electric Horse came up, drawing the attached carriage, with swift, majestic strides, Frank, through the irresistible power of electricity, had put the natives to flight.

The party boarded the vehicle at once, and turning on a good supply of the motive power, Mr. Reade, Sr., caused the whole machine to move off swiftly. **FR**

*Frank Reade Jr. built electric vehicles exclusively—not for environmental reasons, but because he believed in the superiority of electricity as a motive power source.*

*Frank Jr. can be seen peering out of the bird's eye
in this fantasy illustration.*

# RETURN ENGAGEMENT

**F**RANK JR. AND HIS FATHER did collaborate on an Electric Horse, as depicted in *Frank Reade Library #38*, which must've been quite a sight galloping around Readestown. All their robots still suffered from the same limitation, though—they had to be attached to carriages for support. Even the Reades couldn't invent a machine capable of truly walking like a man or a horse.

Frustrated, Frank Jr. turned his attention back to his airship. After testing the *Zephyr* on a few short flights, he was itching to take it on a field mission. He got the perfect opportunity in 1886, and it involved his old adversary Geronimo.

## — CHANGING OF THE GUARD —

**I**N A FINAL BID FOR FREEDOM, Geronimo and about a hundred other Apache had bolted from their reservation in Arizona the year before. Once again, General Crook tracked them down in the Sierra Madre mountains. Geronimo agreed to surrender, then reneged and took off again.

The hunt for Geronimo came to symbolize something much larger—the last stages of conquering the West—and was the talk of the nation. The Apaches' escape got Crook into such hot water, with the press and with his superiors, that he asked to be relieved. His request was promptly granted.

General Nelson Miles took command in May 1886 with a new strategy, deploying thousands of troops in hard pursuit of the renegade Apache, whose numbers had dwindled to a few dozen. Still Geronimo evaded capture.

Frank Jr. avidly followed the news in Readestown, until he couldn't stand it anymore and flew west to offer his services to General Miles.

Gen. George Crook spoke out against the unjust treatment of Native Americans. The Apache called him *Nantan Lupan*, or Grey Wolf, out of respect. Crook spent the last years of his life working to get exiled Apache out of the Southeast, where the climate was killing them, and back into the arid West.

Gen. Nelson Miles replaced Crook, who was considered too soft on the Apache, in the final hunt for Geronimo. Miles had the advantage of Frank Jr.'s first airship being placed at his disposal.

Frank Jr.'s air reconnaissance was instrumental in Geronimo's 1886 capture.

The *Valiant* is depicted as the *Clipper of the Prairie* in this fictionalized account of Frank Jr.'s attempt to capture Geronimo.

# FRANK READE

## WEEKLY MAGAZINE,

### Containing Stories of Adventures on Land, Sea & in the Air.

Issued Weekly—By Subscription $2.50 per year. Application made for Second-Class Entry at N. Y. Post-Office.

No. 39.     NEW YORK, JULY 24, 1903.     Price 5 Cents.

## FRANK READE, JR.'S · CLIPPER · OF THE PRAIRIE; OR, FIGHTING THE APACHES IN THE SOUTHWEST.

By "NONAME"

Frank went to the electric gun. The Apaches came yelling down to the water's edge. They were evidently disposed to resent this invasion of the Clipper and assumed the aggressive. It was a lively scrimmage that followed.

➤ *Crook understands the savages well but is too friendly toward them; Miles is the converse, showing no mercy yet neither any detailed knowledge of the enemy's ways. We shall make short work of this chase in the Zephyr, tracking the Apache from above no matter how forbidding the terrain below.*

JOURNAL OF FRANK READE JR. (JUNE 6, 1886)

## — EYE IN THE SKY —

GENERAL MILES gladly accepted Frank Jr.'s offer. As the young inventor had predicted, he made short work of the search. The *Zephyr* soared gracefully over crags and canyons that would've taken weeks to struggle through on foot. Within days, Frank Jr. spotted a small group of Apache.

Frank Jr. communicated with Miles's ground troops by means of a heliograph, a pre-radio device that uses mirrors to transmit messages over long distances. Again and again, the soldiers were able to take the Apache by surprise and catch a few of them while the rest scattered.

➤ *Adjt.-Gen. Drum received the following telegram from Gen. Miles, dated July 22: "Capt. Lawton reports that his command surprised Geronimo's camp on Yonge River . . . nearly 300 miles south of the Mexican boundary, capturing all the Indian property, including hundreds of pounds of dried meat, and 19 riding animals.*

*"This is the fifth time this month in which the Indians have been surprised by the troops, with the aid of Mr. Reade's aerial reconnaissance. It has given encouragement to the troops and has reduced the number and strength of the Indians, and has given the Indians a feeling of insecurity, even in the remote and almost inaccessible mountains of Mexico."*

"UNPLEASANT FOR GERONIMO," *NEW YORK TIMES*
(JULY 24, 1886)

## — "BROKEN IN SPIRIT" —

AT LAST, in late August, Geronimo and his exhausted band agreed to stop running. They officially surrendered to General Miles on September 4, 1886, and were shipped off to exile in Florida.

➤ *If credit be given to the troops for the courage and endurance which animated them during this campaign, what can be said of their foes? For more than a year they made a running fight through the most rugged and barren portions of the Sierras, without subsistence of any kind except what they could rapidly snatch from the valleys as they swept from mountain to mountain, alternately scorched by the midsummer sun and chilled by the frost of snowclad peaks.*

*Broken in spirit and worn in body, harried from the sky and the ground, they buried the hatchet at the feet of their gallant pursuers. If the strategical skill and physical force manifested against the government by these outlaws can be directed to its advantage, no portion of our military establishment could be more efficient.*

LIEUTENANT MARION P. MAUS, "A CAMPAIGN AGAINST
THE APACHES," IN *PERSONAL RECOLLECTIONS AND
OBSERVATIONS OF GENERAL NELSON A. MILES*
(THE WERNER COMPANY, 1896)

After the surrender, Frank Jr. recorded an apparently baffling dream in his journal.

➤ *Last night in my dreams I traveled with an Apache tribe that committed no acts of savagery, but only hunted game and danced about a great bonfire under the stars. I felt contented in the dream but discomfited upon waking. I know not what this signifies.*

JOURNAL OF FRANK READE JR. (SEPTEMBER 6, 1886)

✫✫

Apache dancers as *Gaan* spirits.

Other Indian Campaigns: Pequot War 1637
King Philip's War 1675–1676
Chickamauga War 1776–1794
Red Stick War 1813–1814
Peoria War 1813
Winnebago War 1827

Bannock War 1878

Cheyenne War 1878 – 1879

Pine Ridge Campaign 1890 – 1891

Nez Perce War 1877

Black Hills War 1876 – 1877

Modoc War 1872 – 1873

Ute War 1879 – 1880

Black Hawk War 1832

Northwest Indian War 1790 – 1795

Comanche Campaign 1867 – 1875

Tecumseh's Rebellion 1811

Apache Wars 1873 1885 – 1886

Adobe Walls 1874

Creek War 1813 – 1814 1836 – 1837

Geronimo 1883 1886

Seminole Wars 1817 – 1818 1835 – 1842 1855 – 1858

**Indian Campaign Medal
United States Army**

Eligibility limited to fourteen designated military campaigns
1790 - 1891

⭐ Frank Reade Jr. conflicts

Texas–Indian Wars 1836–1875
Cayuse War 1848–1855
Mariposa War 1850–1851
Yuma War 1851–1852
Apache Campaigns 1854–1900
Klamath River War 1855
Puget Sound War 1855–1856
Rogue River War 1855–1856
Yakima War 1855–1858
Navajo Wars 1858–1864
Bald Hills War 1858–1865
Paiute War 1860
Dakota War 1862
Colorado War 1863–1865
Snake War 1864–1869
Hualapai War 1865–1870
Red Cloud's War 1866–1868
Red River War 1874
Sheepeater Campaign 1879

# AMERICAN
## HOLOCAUST

**M**ILLIONS of Native Americans were killed or forcibly relocated and reeducated during the nineteenth century. Many historians assert that their treatment fits the definition of genocide.

Even before the Indian Removal Act of 1830 was passed, the U.S. government was systematically displacing Indians from their ancestral homelands. Methods ranged from the legal, which included unfair treaties and lopsided laws, to the lethal, such as forced marches of entire tribes and the slaughter of whole villages.

The resulting series of conflicts between Native Americans and new Americans spanned a century and is now called the Indian Wars. To fight an enemy military force that had superior firepower and numbers, Native Americans resorted to guerrilla and terror tactics. Sadly, this set off cycles of vengeful atrocities, stoking white anger and, in some people's eyes, proving that the "savages" should be exterminated. The most infamous act of savagery often associated with Native Americans—scalping—was actually started by whites.

The Battle of Adobe Walls and Apache campaigns in which Frank Reade Jr. fought were part of these cycles, as Indians were squeezed onto ever smaller reservations, mistreated by corrupt agents, and hunted when they fled.

➤ *[T]he long struggle between the government and the Apache Indians . . . bears all the earmarks of a traditional, or secessionist, insurgency . . . The experience of the U.S. Government with the Apaches confirms the validity of much of our current doctrine, and offers lessons which can be applied to modern counterinsurgency operations.*

MAJOR JACQUE J. STEWART,
"THE U.S. GOVERNMENT AND THE APACHE INDIANS 1871–1876: A CASE STUDY IN COUNTERINSURGENCY" (U.S. ARMY COMMAND AND GENERAL STAFF COLLEGE, 1993) ★★

This statue—*The Rescue, or Daniel Boone Saves His Family*—stood outside the entrance of the U.S. Capitol from 1853 until 1958. Every president from Franklin Pierce to Dwight Eisenhower was sworn into office in front of this oversized allegory, which was created to "commemorate the dangers & difficulty of peopling our continent . . . the triumph of the whites over the savage tribes." Dropped by a crane while being moved in 1976, it now sits in pieces at a Smithsonian storage facility.

Dark regions show the precipitous decrease in Native American lands from the founding of the United States to the closing of the American frontier.

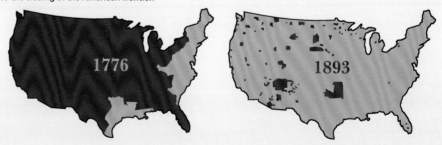

1776

1893

# WESTERN ADVENTURES

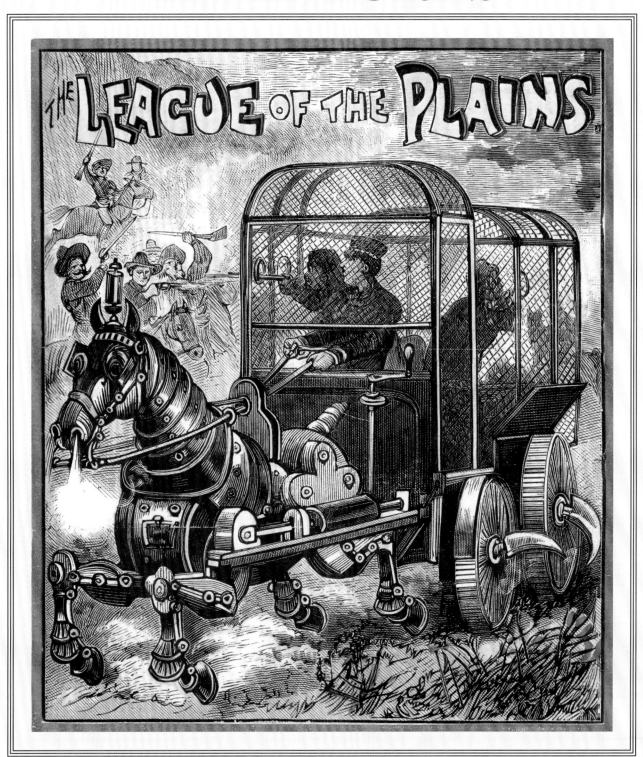

## Frank Reade Jr.'s
# CLIPPER OF THE PRAIRIE
*— or —*
## FIGHTING THE APACHES IN THE FAR SOUTHWEST
*Frank Reade Library #87*

### CHAPTER IV
### *The Apaches Cornered*

The Apaches were now in overwhelming force. From every part they concentrated in the Valley of Desolation. They were massing from all quarters and now came sweeping down through the valley in three divisions.

Frank saw that a critical time had come. He went forward in the *Clipper* and trained its electric gun upon the distant body of horsemen, taking the center as an objective mark. Then he sent a dynamite projectile hurtling over the plain.

At the moment the foe were distant over half a mile. But Frank's aim was true, and the projectile struck in their front rank. The effect was indescribable. Horses and riders were thrown high in the air. Others were hurled right and left like puppets. A mighty hole was blown in the ground.

Again Frank trained the wonderful electric gun. Again a projectile burst in the midst of the terrified body of Indians. A score of them were killed. They broke and fled in wild confusion. They were unable to understand the nature of the terrific death balls hurled at them.

So the charge upon the *Clipper* was dispelled like mist before the sun. Those on board the machine cheered lustily over their victory.

Frank's face still wore the same grim smile. "What did I tell you?" he said, coolly, as Vane gripped his hand. "I knew that I could drive them to a retreat."

"And so you did!" cried the young sergeant, excitedly. "It was a grand victory! I have all confidence in the ability of the *Clipper* to whip an army!"

## CHAPTER V
### *A Parley With Alchise*

Daylight came at last. There were numbers of the Apaches slain upon the plain. But not a living savage was in sight. All was quiet on the cliff, and their presence might have been doubted, but for a signal fire.

Near the hour of noon a white flag was seen to appear over the rampart above. Frank stepped out upon the platform of the *Clipper,* and answered the signal by holding up his hands.

Then down the face of the cliff slid a little Apache. He came on until he stood upon the plain at the base of the cliff. A few more reassuring signals and he advanced toward the *Clipper.*

When within speaking distance Frank addressed him in Mexican: "Well, my red friend, what will you have?"

The Apache regarded Frank steadily for a moment, and then replied: "The great chief Alchise asks for a council with you. He will meet you at the foot of the cliff."

"Tell him I will meet him there!" said Frank.

The messenger turned and bounded away like an arrow. A few moments later Alchise himself and two of his chiefs was seen coming down the path.

Frank said to Vane: "Come with me!" They left the *Clipper* and set out to meet the Apaches.

Alchise halted just in the shadow of a clump of mesquite. He folded his arms and maintained a dignified attitude as the two white men came up. He bowed stiffly in answer to Frank's salutation. One of his chiefs acted as interpreter.

"Alchise," said Frank, sternly, "you are doing wrong in making war upon the white man. You know that well."

This was interpreted to the famous chief. His lip curled in scorn. "Why does the Apache make war upon his white brother?" he cried, scornfully. "Shall he ask that question? Who shall pay for the cornfields taken from our people on the Gila? Who forced us to take abode in the fever regions of the San Carlos, where our braves sicken and die and our squaws mourn? Who shall defend the Apache but himself?"

In a measure, Frank and Vane both knew that the Indian was right.

It is a stain upon the honor of this country that the greed for gain of a few unscrupulous individuals should have led to the appropriation of those lands which were really the property of the Apache, and where he was happy and content. But we will indulge in no homily upon the government's Indian policy, or the injustice therefrom accruing.

"You have been dealt wrongly with beyond doubt," said Frank, in a kindly tone; "but you are making war upon those people who are entirely innocent of wronging you. You cannot hope to gain justice in that way."

"My white brother speaks soft words!" replied Alchise. "So have all before him done. But he cannot blind the Apache again. We will die in our rights."

"That is a brave resolution," replied Frank, "but how futile. It is better to be at peace with the white man who is more powerful than you."

"Why shall you speak of peace?" cried Alchise, angrily. "Look upon my people. They are driven from their hunting grounds. The buffalo has passed into the happy hunting grounds for the Indian now. He too must pass to the great beyond with the buffalo!" There was something like a vein of sadness in the chief's voice. A shadow passed over his strong face.

Frank hardly knew how to meet these arguments of the chief. "Then you will not talk of peace?" he asked, finally.

**FR**

FRANK READE, JR.'S PRAIRIE WHIRLWIND; OR, THE MYSTERY OF THE HIDDEN CANYON.

# FRANK • READE

## WEEKLY MAGAZINE,

### Containing Stories of Adventures on Land, Sea & in the Air.

Issued Weekly—By Subscription $2.50 per year.  Application made for Second-Class Entry at N. Y. Post Office.

**No. 76.**          **NEW YORK, APRIL 8, 1904.**          **Price 5 Cents.**

ADRIFT·IN·ASIA
WITH FRANK READE, JR.
*By "NONAME".*

The Sky Pilot had risen a few hundred feet when a startling and unlooked-for thing occurred. Suddenly the blended reports of rifles was heard.  Bullets came rattling against the airship's hull.  It was a close call for Beals.

# 3
# AGE *of*
# EXPANSION

AFTER HIS LAST APACHE ADVENTURE, which knocked Geronimo off the warpath once and for all, it looked like Frank Reade Jr. might settle down at last. But just as the United States started to run out of frontier within its borders and cast an appraising glance at other lands, he too started looking for overseas opportunities. Try as he might, Frank Jr. couldn't stay put for long.

Frank Reade Jr. with his daughter, Kate.

## INTO *the* HEART *of* DARKNESS

FRANK JR. WAS IN LONDON when news broke that his boyhood hero Henry Morton Stanley, a writer and adventurer famed for exploring uncharted regions of Africa, had gone missing. Stanley's books *How I Found Livingstone* (1871) and *Through the Dark Continent* (1878), dog-eared from years of perusal, occupied a prized spot in Frank Jr.'s library.

➤ *My clever little Kate! I do not like to see her shed a tear when I depart. Still, it is a great comfort to know that her shining smile will greet my return.*

*Mother chides me for not allowing Emilie and the children to accompany me on expeditions. She does not comprehend the world's many evils—she and Father choose to see only its most civilized parts and always to think the best of people. They are naïve.*

*I have a duty to bring light to the dark lands, but never would I put my family in peril. If being separated from them at times is the price I must pay, then so be it. They shall keep safe with Father and his construction projects.*

JOURNAL OF FRANK READE JR.
(OCTOBER 4, 1887)

HENRY M. STANLEY

Henry Morton Stanley was a writer, explorer, and self-promoter, best known for tracking down a missing Scottish missionary named David Livingstone in Africa. He was the perfect candidate to help King Leopold II claim the Congo. Stanley's expeditions became infamous for their brutality toward both the native population and his own porters and officers. That didn't keep him from being elected to England's Parliament in 1895.

On his latest adventure, Stanley had vanished into the dense Ituri rain forest, into which no white man and few Africans had ever ventured. No one had heard from him in months. The expedition was a big story in England, where there was much conjecture about Stanley's fate.

◆ *The dark continent, which Mr. Stanley has done so much to make us acquainted with, hides him from us at present in her innermost recesses. Speculation is rife not only as to his whereabouts, but even as to his being alive. Mystery always enshrouds the doings and fate of him who ventures beyond those gloomy barriers of forest, mountain, swamp and river, which screen Central Africa from even the faint and reflected gleams of civilization. I have faith that the luminosity of Mr. Reade's science can penetrate this Stygian realm.*

GENERAL VISCOUNT GARNET JOSEPH WOLSELEY, "IS STANLEY DEAD?" *THE NORTH AMERICAN REVIEW,* VOL. 147, NO. 385 (DECEMBER 1887)

## —— HERO WORSHIP ——

CONGO.
FEMME DU CONGO.

**M**EETING YOUR HEROES in person is a big gamble. If you win, it's like touching a god. Lose, and your dreams are shattered. Frank Jr. decided to take that bet.

The young inventor was thrilled when King Leopold II of Belgium, who employed Stanley and owned the Congo Free State, asked him to help find Stanley. But the reasons Frank Jr. gave in a letter to his wife stood in marked contrast to his private journal.

◆ *Dearest—It cheers me to know that you and the children are enjoying Paris with Mother, since it is now likely that I shall not return before Christmas. An opportunity has arisen for me to be of service in locating the eminent explorer Mr. Henry M. Stanley in the Congo. We are then to complete his mission of* relieving Emin Pasha, the besieged governor of the neighboring Sudanese province of Equatoria, who has captured the newspapers' attention of late. I go at the behest of Belgium's Leopold himself.

FRANK READE JR., LETTER TO EMILIE READE (OCTOBER 4, 1887)

◆ *When he spies the White Cruiser coming to his aid, surely Stanley will cry, "At last, a worthy partner!" He and I together could solve the mysteries of Darkest Africa and map the farthest reaches of the Earth. Oh, we shall laugh at that old Leopold—the scoundrel!—who tried to flatter me into giving him the secrets to my flying ships. Evidently His Majesty is accustomed to having his way, for he was ill pleased when I refused.*

JOURNAL OF FRANK READE JR. (OCTOBER 4, 1887)

## —— BULA MATARI ——

**B**EFORE MARCHING into the unknown Ituri jungle, Stanley spent three months traveling up the Congo River with a huge force of nearly eight hundred men. Although woefully short on basic supplies, they had plenty of ammunition and attitude. If local tribes refused

died of fever, or gone back to Zanzibar, or joined forces with slave traders), Frank Jr. plunged into the jungle after him.

The natives didn't offer much help, for reasons Pompei especially empathized with.

◆ *All our interpreter's skill can scarce cajole the natives to palaver with us, and even my presence don't calm them down much. I can't say as I blame them. They may be primitives to us, but they are no fools. If they speak truth, which I believe they do, Mr. Stanley's party kidnapped their womenfolk and burnt down their village. Ain't no excuse for that.*

POMPEI DUSABLE, LETTER TO ANNIE DUSABLE (NOVEMBER 12, 1887)

According to Frank Jr., Pomp was violently upset by what they learned about Stanley's misdeeds.

◆ *I've sent Pomp ahead in the **White Cruiser** to meet us at Lake Albert. It won't do to let him get too riled up, or he'll start picking fights with our Irish brawler!*

JOURNAL OF FRANK READE JR. (NOVEMBER 15, 1887)

Stanley drastically underestimated how quickly he would be able to traverse parts of the Congo. An expedition that he thought would take months instead stretched into years. The nearly impenetrable jungle shown here was only one of many obstacles.

Frank Reade Jr. departs from London in the *White Cruiser* on his mission to find Henry M. Stanley. The inventor also took along his amphibious all-terrain vehicle the *Boomerang.* Dime-novel depictions of Frank Jr.'s adventures show him deploying a veritable fleet of fantastic vehicles in Africa.

to offer food or shelter, Stanley—whose nickname in Kikongo, *Bula Matari,* means Breaker of Stones—would attack and take whatever he could grab.

Frank Jr. and his crew speedily retraced the river route in their amphibious rover *Boomerang,* seeking clues to Stanley's whereabouts. Finding nothing but conflicting rumors (Stanley had

## "MR. STANLEY, I PRESUME?" —

Hiram Maxim himself gave a prototype of his newly invented Maxim machine gun to Stanley's expedition. The powerful weapon would become a standard fixture in colonial warfare for decades to come.

WITH HIS high-tech ATV, Frank Jr. had no trouble plowing through the Ituri jungle at a speed that Stanley could only have dreamt of. Native warriors' poison-tipped arrows and pit traps, which had plagued Stanley's men, were no match for the *Boomerang's* armored hull. The only dilemma was how to find the lost explorer.

After a few days of zigzagging through the jungle, Frank Jr. came across evidence of a recent European-style encampment. From there, he followed a grisly trail of dead or dying porters until, on December 10, he came face-to-face with his hero.

Curiously, Stanley doesn't mention Frank Jr. anywhere in his thousand-page book about the expedition. Then again, it's not unusual for Stanley's version of events to differ from everyone else's. More unusual is the fact that a dozen pages were torn out of Frank Jr.'s journal, covering precisely the period of their meeting. We have only Barney's description of their first encounter.

➤ *Henry Morton Stanley is an ass. He brays at every one and insists he don't need rescuing, when it's plain to see that we reached him in the very nick. The darkys were set to skin him alive for setting fire to a whole valley. It's rescuing him we are, and taking him to Lake Albert, like it or not. For a moment, I thought*

Stanley's men occupied and/or destroyed uncooperative villages, seizing whatever provisions they could find.

*I saw Mister Frank looking as if he'd just been slapped by the Almighty himself, but the next minute he was right as a trivet.*

BARNEY O'SHEA, LETTER TO BETTY O'SHEA
(DECEMBER 10, 1887)

The next entry in Frank Jr.'s journal comes several days later and makes only a passing reference to Stanley.

➤ *Yesterday we arrived at Lake Albert, where faithful Pomp awaited us with my air ship. There is, however, no sign of Emin Pasha. Stanley plans to trek back to Ibwiri and build a fort there.*

JOURNAL OF FRANK READE JR. (DECEMBER 15, 1887)

Arthur Jephson, one of Stanley's officers on the expedition, provides a revealing account in his posthumously published diary.

➤ *Mr. Reade has delivered us from a waking nightmare. To say one experienced a feeling of relief or even of joy on at last seeing the Lake would hardly describe what one felt. The Lake had ever been the goal held up before one's eyes since we had left Yambuya, nearly 6 months ago. In our first dark days we had always looked to it as the haven where all our troubles would end. Yet our feelings of triumph and gratitude are tempered by the knowledge that we left Yambuya with 389 men and arrived on the shores of the Albert with 169 only. The difference between the two numbers speaks for itself.*

JOURNAL OF ARTHUR J. M. JEPHSON
(DECEMBER 15, 1887)

## — A PARTING OF THE WAYS —

It would be another four months until the bedraggled remnants of Stanley's advance column finally made contact with Emin Pasha. To their deep annoyance, he didn't want to be rescued, either. The German-born Emin was enjoying life in Africa and mainly wanted to be left alone to collect nature specimens.

That was the last straw for Frank Jr. He went his own way and was out of Africa long before Stanley.

***This is the last time I shall act in the service of a foreign power. The entire undertaking would be a farce, were it not such a monumental waste of money and men. The Pasha vacillates and refuses to recognize that his situation is now even more precarious, the Mahdists having been stirred to rebellion again by Stanley's incursion. There is no helping a man who refuses to help himself. We are leaving them all to their own devices and to God's grace.***

Journal of Frank Reade Jr. (May 8, 1888)

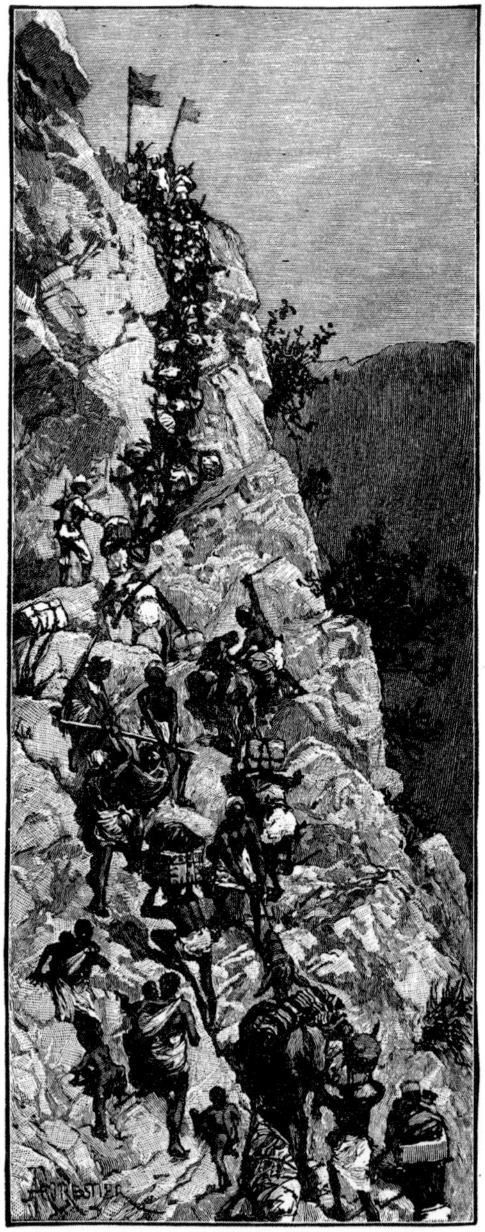

More than seven hundred porters carried the supplies of Stanley's expedition in single-file lines that stretched for miles across inhospitable terrain. In the end, fewer than two hundred porters were left.

As for Stanley's vaunted relief expedition, it took another year for him to retrieve what was left of its rear column, browbeat Emin Pasha into leaving, and march his weary survivors to the east coast of Africa. In the end, Emin wound up staying in Africa, serving as a colonel in the German army until he was killed in 1892. Stanley went back to England without him in 1890.

***None of us was sorry to see the last of Mr. Stanley, and the boss brightened up soon as we moved on to exploring for our own sake. Mr. Frank done found some diamonds big as hen eggs—that man has got a nose for treasure!***

Pompei DuSable, letter to Annie DuSable (May 23, 1888)

## — JUNGLE FEVER —

Many years later, this all came as news to Kate Reade, who was only a toddler in 1887. Kate complained to her friend Texas Guinan about Frank Jr.'s claim that he'd never been in the Congo, calling him "one big lie, from start to finish."

***You remember all that fuss about the Congo back in 1905 or so? Papa was there during that horrid Leopold's rule. I used to pester him about taking me to Africa, because I thought the dog-faced men were real when I was little. He told me all those dime novel stories were made up, that he never went near Africa.***

Kate Reade, letter to Texas Guinan (January 29, 1933)

Guinan had a more forgiving, perhaps more worldly, view.

***Try not to be so tough on your dad, kiddo. So he told you he was never in Africa. What if you went through Hell on earth to rescue someone you idolized, only to find out he was the Devil himself, and you had to go through***

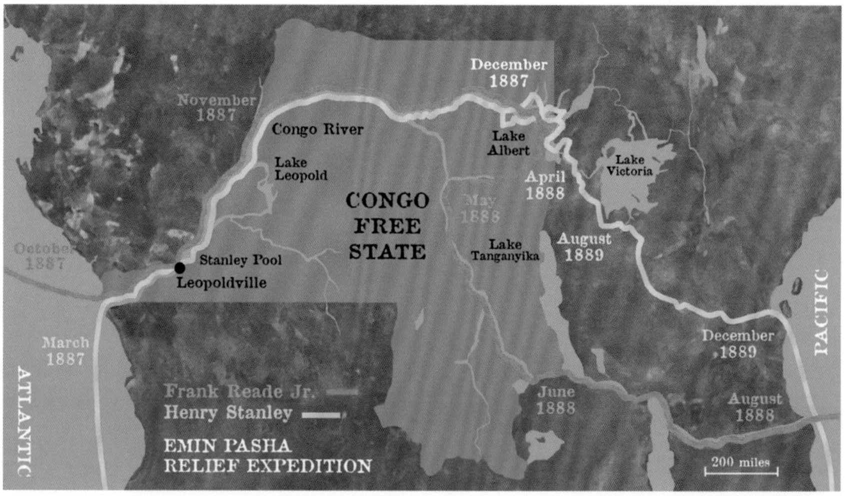

*Hell all over again just to get away from him? You wouldn't want to talk about it either. And you'd never be able to forget it.*

TEXAS GUINAN, LETTER TO KATE READE (FEBRUARY 18, 1933)

The Reade family never talked about Frank Jr.'s time in Africa, even though—or maybe because—the experience haunted him for the rest of his life.

◆ *Another damned nightmare about the Congo. Lost in a sweltering jungle of perpetual twilight, heaps of men dying of every imaginable tropical ailment, women and children with no hands being cruelly beaten, and I became the one doling out beatings. Curse that Conrad for dredging it all up from the black depths.*

JOURNAL OF FRANK READE JR. (NOVEMBER 7, 1900)

☆ ☆

Emin Pasha was governor of Equatoria, a southern province of Sudan under Anglo-Egyptian control. In 1885, a native Sudanese rebellion cut off Equatoria from the outside world, and the popular British general Charles Gordon was killed in a nearby province. After the British press published a letter from Emin and took to calling him "Gordon's last lieutenant," English pride demanded his rescue. A relief expedition was formed, led by Henry M. Stanley. By the time Stanley reached Emin two years later, the crisis had abated, and the governor didn't want to leave.

# THE
# CONGO
## FREE STATE

**A**S THE SCRAMBLE for Africa heated up in the late nineteenth century, European powers carved up the continent but left unclaimed a massive section in its center. The territory was deemed economically unimportant, and the terrain was practically impassible. But King Leopold II, of the tiny country of Belgium, desperately wanted a colony—and he set his sights on the Congo, deep in the African interior.

King Leopold II of Belgium privately owned the Congo Free State from 1885 until 1908, presiding over the deaths of ten million souls.

### — HOW TO STEAL A COUNTRY —

**L**EOPOLD CREATED a front organization called the International African Association, ostensibly for humanitarian and scientific purposes. He hired the well-known adventurer Henry Stanley to explore the region and obtain concessions from local tribes, who had no idea what they were signing away. Eventually trading posts were established, and a private paramilitary called the *Force Publique* (Public Force) was organized.

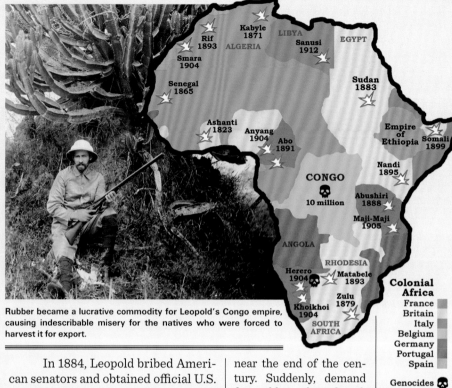

Rubber became a lucrative commodity for Leopold's Congo empire, causing indescribable misery for the natives who were forced to harvest it for export.

**Colonial Africa**
France
Britain
Italy
Belgium
Germany
Portugal
Spain

Genocides 💀

Resistance campaigns prior to World War I

In 1884, Leopold bribed American senators and obtained official U.S. recognition of his claim to the Congo. He placated European rivals with false promises of a profitable "free trade" zone. The king now owned the largest privately held land in world history, measuring nearly a million square miles. He named it the Congo Free State.

The king garnered international public support by claiming that his goals were altruistic: opening the Congo to researchers, bringing civilization to the locals, and protecting natives against the so-called Arab slave trade. Many of the Arab slave traders were actually Africans who wore Arabic clothing and sold their captives in Arab markets. Western press and politicians were already busily decrying the Arab slave trade, providing easy justification for the notion that Europeans had to save Africans from foreign powers.

### — THE RUBBER KING —

**L**EOPOLD'S TRUE GOAL was, of course, to extract as much personal wealth as possible from his new property. At first, ivory was a big moneymaker. His best opportunity unexpectedly came out of science, when the pneumatic tire and electrical insulation were developed near the end of the century. Suddenly, demand for rubber skyrocketed, turning the rubber plants that grew wild in the Congo into a very lucrative commodity. The rubber trade made the king dazzlingly wealthy, but at a terrible cost in human suffering.

Harvesting rubber from wild vines is slow, arduous work. To collect the large amounts needed for international trade, the king's private police conscripted native villagers as unwilling laborers. Using violence and terror, the Force Publique would force each village to meet a rubber quota. Printed handbooks gave instructions on how native wives and children were to be held hostage, and whole communities destroyed, to compel cooperation. Villagers were also expected to provide food and materials for the regional outpost's soldiers and administrators, even though the rubber harvesting work left them no time for farming.

A cartoon poking fun at Leopold's penchant for young mistresses. Then, as now, sex scandals often distracted public attention from weightier issues.

Congolese with severed hands, living evidence of the atrocities perpetrated under Leopold's reign.

Punishment for Congolese refusing or failing to meet rubber quotas was death. Because European officers didn't trust their African subordinates, *Force Publique* soldiers were ordered to bring in a severed human hand for each shot fired, as proof of the kill. The victims were not, however, always dead. Quotas kept escalating, and before long, baskets full of severed hands were being delivered to post commanders. A soldier could shorten his tour of duty by turning in more hands. The grisly tokens became a kind of currency, which led to even more widespread atrocities.

## OUT OF THE FRYING PAN

**A**LL OF THIS, and more, was painstakingly uncovered by a shipping office clerk named Edmund Morel. He grew suspicious of the Congo Free State when he noticed that although many vessels left the Congo laden with rubber and other marketable resources, most of the goods being shipped into the Congo were guns, ammunition, explosives, and chains to be used by the state's police. This was not "trade" by anyone's definition.

Medal given by King Leopold II for service in the Congo.

Morel quit his job and devoted his life to exposing the horrors of the Congo. In 1902, Joseph Conrad's novel *Heart of Darkness* (later the basis for the film *Apocalypse Now*) graphically depicted life under the hellish regime and its brutal practices. Arthur Conan Doyle and Mark Twain, among others, lent their celebrity to the cause of liberating the Congo. It became the first international humanitarian relief movement.

Leon Rom, a former Belgian soldier, commanded a remote outpost in Leopold's Congo. He became head of the territory's private army, the Force Publique. Rom's psychopathic approach to governance, which included displaying severed human heads as garden decorations on the grounds of his offices, was an inspiration for Col. Kurtz in the novel *Heart of Darkness*. Rom's display would later be referenced in the film adaptation, *Apocalypse Now*, when Dennis Hopper says to Martin Sheen, "You're looking at the heads . . . sometimes he goes too far."

Years after public outrage rose to a fever pitch, Belgium took control of the Congo from King Leopold in 1908. By then, ten million Congolese had been killed under his rule.

Fifty years later, the Congo gained independence, and the people elected reform-minded Patrice Lumumba as prime minister. Lumumba didn't play ball with military or mining interests, though, and was killed in a CIA-backed coup endorsed by U.S. President Dwight Eisenhower. After General Mobutu Sese Seko took power and renamed the country Zaire, the Congo slid back into despotism.

The discovery of oil there has only raised the stakes. Now known as the Democratic Republic of the Congo, the region is still wracked by patterns of violence and exploitation established more than a century ago. ★★

Police headquarters of the ironically named Congo Free State. The colonial force was instructed by its administrators to use terror tactics in controlling local residents.

# FRANK READE

## WEEKLY MAGAZINE.

### Containing Stories of Adventures on Land, Sea & in the Air.

Issued Weekly—By Subscription $2.50 per year    Application made for Second-Class Entry at N Y. Post-Office.

No. 12.      NEW YORK, JANUARY 16, 1903.      Price 5 Cents.

# FIGHTING THE SLAVE HUNTERS;
## OR, FRANK READE, JR., IN CENTRAL AFRICA.
### By "NONAME."

Down through the line of M'bokis went the Vendetta. Frank tried hard to reach the white traders.
If he could have done so. he would gladly have crushed them also  But
Hardinger and his gang foresaw their peril.

# AFRICAN ADVENTURES

## Frank Reade Jr.'s
# WHITE CRUISER
### OF THE CLOUDS
— or —
### THE SEARCH FOR THE
# DOG-FACED MEN
*Frank Reade Library #21*

### CHAPTER VI
### *A Friendly Tribe*

Suddenly the forest began to give way to a lovely little valley right down in the heart of the wild region. It was a perfect Eden, and as they entered it Frank exclaimed: "I never saw the equal of this before. This must have been the home of Adam and Eve!"

The village of the Mamby tribe now came into view. It was a large collection of several hundred straw thatched huts. As the king's party approached with their distinguished visitors the inhabitants of the town rushed out in a body. Loud shouting and beating of drums followed.

King Loa issued trumpet orders, and in a jiffy the whole concourse formed a square in the center of the town with the visitors and the king in the center. Then a number of stout men lifted bodily the roof of a hut upon four upright posts and placed it over them to shut out the hot rays of the sun. Mats made of rushes were laid upon the ground. Upon these the visitors sat.

The king's orders were given quick and sharp and instantly obeyed. A buffalo calf was led forth and killed, and in a jiffy its carcass was dexterously dressed and cooking over a bed of hot coals. Drink was brought the visitors in gourds, and presently men came up tugging heavy tusks of ivory, one of which was laid at the feet of each guest as a gift.

The drink was a peculiar kind of wine, manufactured partly from the cocoanut and was very refreshing. Pomp took to it kindly, with the result that it made his tongue more glib than ever. His opinion of the "po' trash" began to undergo a decided change. They were now to his thinking "very fine gen'lemen."

RUSH OF THE DWARFS

### CHAPTER VII
### *Jedediah Distinguishes Himself*

Frank turned to the native king and asked: "King Loa, in all this region, have you ever heard of a race of men who have faces shaped like a dog's?"

The king's face lit up. "Nautchi Mba," he said. "Yes, they are our foes." King Loa then proceeded to give Frank valuable information.

His description was most graphic and interesting. According to it, the Nautchi Mba or dog-faced men were a frightful race of cannibals and wild men. They were the deadly enemies of all other tribes, and in battle they were fierce and invincible. Of all the savages in Central Africa, they were by far the most blood-thirsty.

Frank listened to this description with deepest interest. According to King Loa's declaration the Mamby village was even now threatened by an attack from the Nautchi Mba. The king was much worried about it, and feared that the wretches would sweep his little band out of existence.

Frank's sympathy was aroused. "They shall not do it!" he declared. "Fear not, King Loa! I will help you!"

Without delay, the three explorers started for the *White Cruiser*. Its rotascopes were just visible over a rise of land, so they knew that it was still where they had left it.

But at this moment a thrilling incident happened. Distant rifle shots were heard, and then the air-ship was seen to leap into the air.

"Barney has been attacked!" cried Frank, in alarm.

Sure enough, the dog-faced men had attacked the air-ship. And now from the cover of a clump of palms a gang of them were seen rushing toward our adventurers. For a moment our friends were utterly paralyzed.

The appearance of the strange barbarians was something frightful. They were literal giants in frame and stature, with long, black hair covering head and face and the upper part of the body. Their heads were of an abnormal size, seeming as large as those of lions, and they carried huge spears and battle clubs.

A hand-to-hand conflict with the Nautchi Mba in such numbers as they were was little short of suicidal. But Frank looked up to see where the air-ship was.

To his joy he saw the *White Cruiser* descending toward them, and

Barney at the rail letting down a long rope ladder. This fell at their feet. In a moment Frank grasped it, crying: "Come, boys, get hold here! It is our only hope!"

The dog-faced men were coming down the slope like a whirlwind. There was no time to lose. Jedediah sprang up onto the ladder. Pomp followed him. Then Barney sent the air-ship up. Up from the ground, clinging to the rope ladder, went the three men. It was a narrow escape. **FR**

Kate could operate any of the Reades' steam equipment at an early age.

Frank Jr. brought these zebras back from Africa as a gift for his wife, Emilie.

# ROBOT RIVAL

**A**FTER RETURNING to Readestown from Africa in 1889, Frank Jr. stayed closer to home for a few years, designing new vehicles and occasionally poking at his robotics research. Kate has fond memories of this period.

➤ *That was the first time I clearly remember Papa coming home. We did experiments in wireless telegraphy together, and he made a pedal-powered miniature* **Valiant** *for me. And those ridiculous zebras he gave to Mama—now I know he must've carted them back all the way from Africa!*

JOURNAL OF KATE READE
(APRIL 21, 1933)

➤ *Kate is so very happy to have her Papa back! She adores our air-ship tours. Last week we flew all the way to Florida, where we marveled at the palm trees and alligators and the many birds with long, sinuous necks.*

JOURNAL OF EMILIE READE (JANUARY 13, 1889)

Frank Jr. kept up an occasional correspondence with Archie Campion, but didn't take his research too seriously. In 1893, Archie sent Frank Jr. word of a new invention that changed his mind. The whole Reade family flew to Chicago to see it at the World's Columbian Exposition.

➤ *In return for your generosity in allowing me to tour Readeworks, I hope you and your family will do me the honor of being our guests in Chicago during the Fair and attending a demonstration of my mechanical man.*

ARCHIBALD CAMPION, LETTER TO FRANK READE JR.
(MAY 26, 1893)

Kate Reade, c. 1890.

The Reade family home, designed by Frank Sr. with the new architectural firm of Burnham and Root in 1873, was situated within walking distance of the Readeworks factory buildings. The house's observation turret and numerous flagpoles are indicative of the family's predilections.

Partly inspired by Frank Jr.'s Electric Man, Professor Campion's Boilerplate was the world's first robot soldier.

## WONDER OF THE WHITE CITY

ARCHIE had gone into scientific seclusion not long after visiting Readeworks. Upon emerging, he invited the public to meet his greatest creation: Professor Campion's Mechanical Marvel, later known to the world as Boilerplate. Unlike the Reades' electric automata, Boilerplate could walk without any extra support, pick up objects, even follow spoken orders and answer abstract questions. It was a quantum leap in robotics, an achievement that hasn't been matched to this day.

➤ *I congratulate you on your victory, sir; you have done what I could not. You will be pleased to learn that we at Readeworks intend not to compete with you, but rather to concentrate on our specialties, flying machines and electrical vessels, which fall outside your area of expertise.*

FRANK READE JR., LETTER TO ARCHIBALD CAMPION
(JULY 17, 1893)

The Reades knew they would never catch up. They shut down the robotics division of Readeworks, and Frank Sr. went into semiretirement. Jack Wright reported in a letter to his sister, "Boss came home from Chicago and tore up all his Electric Man designs. He says we're done making metal men."

Despite Frank Jr.'s wounded pride, he and Archie became fast friends. Each may have envied and valued in the other certain qualities found lacking

A souvenir ribbon from Machinery Hall, where Archie Campion demonstrated his robot for the Reades and the general public.

in himself—Archie's calm, steadfast dedication to a single goal, versus Frank Jr.'s brash, impulsive style. They exchanged many letters over the decades, and Archie often hitched a ride on one of the Reades' helicopter airships during his world travels with Boilerplate. Archie's sister, Lily, also developed a friendship with Kate Reade, despite the difference in their ages.

➤ *Thank you for your kind hospitality in Chicago. It is such an impressive machine your brother has built! I do believe Frank is jealous. The children were absolutely enchanted by the fair, and Kate is still talking about you.*

EMILIE READE,
LETTER TO LILY CAMPION
(JULY 16, 1893)

✦✦

The Reades' Steam Men became obsolete in the wake of Boilerplate, a fully bipedal robot powered by fuel cells.

Archie Campion and Boilerplate as depicted in a 2010 comic book.

## Jack Wright and His King of the Clouds

Or, Around the World On Wings.
By "NONAME."

Leaning out of the window Jack shouted down at them: "If you don't clear out of there we will fire down at you!" A defiant shout came from the desperadoes, and several of them aimed their rifles up at the machine and fired.

JACK'S CLEVER TRICK.

# JACK WRIGHT and ELECTRIC BOB

To meet reader demand for more Frank Reade dime novels, the Reades' lead designer and fabricator, Jack Wright, was given his own adventure series that ran for years.

**W**HILE FRANK JR. traveled the world with Pompei and Barney, Jack Wright and Electric Bob held down the fort at Readeworks. The two engineers' temperaments weren't suited for adventuring, but they were ideal department heads who took pride in their roles at the company. Without their contributions, Frank Jr. wouldn't have been able to produce nearly as many craft or travel as much as he did.

Jack Wright was a teenager when he met Frank Sr. at the Centennial Exposition in Philadelphia. Jack demonstrated his ability to fabricate any machine part in record time. Frank Sr., who had been struggling to complete his electric gunboat *Centennial* before 1876

Vol. I. { FRANK TOUSEY, Nos. 34 & 36 North Moore St. } NEW YORK, OCTOBER 20, 1894. { $2.50 PER ANNUM, IN ADVANCE. $1.25 FOR SIX MONTHS. } No. 1

## JACK WRIGHT, AND FRANK READE, JR., The Two Young Inventors; or, BRAINS AGAINST BRAINS.

Although Jack Wright and Frank Reade Jr. were coworkers and friends in real life, their fictional counterparts were cast as rivals.

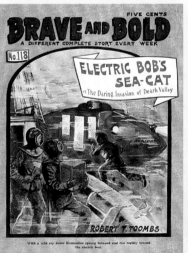

Electric Bob, the Reades' top electrical engineer, also appeared in several magazines as a fictionalized adventurer.

came to a close, hired Jack on the spot. In a few weeks, Jack produced the parts that Readeworks would've taken months to make.

Jack was the company's lead fabricator by 1880, at age twenty. Frank Jr. put him in charge of building vehicles, and Readeworks began to turn out large-scale, high-tech craft at an astounding rate.

Electric Bob, born Robert Brix in 1865, was an apprentice at Readeworks during construction of the *Centennial*. Thanks to his electrical skills, he moved up the ranks quickly. When Frank Jr. built the Electric Man in 1885, Bob was his chief electrician.

Jack and Bob worked for Readeworks until their retirement in the 1920s. Each appeared in fictional dime-novel stories, spinoffs of *Frank Reade Library*, even though they were homebodies in real life. In the early 1930s, Kate Reade brought Electric Bob out of retirement to help with top-secret military projects at her Pearl Harbor base. ★★

# Jack Wright and His Ship of the Desert
Or, Adventures in the Sea of Sand.
BY "NONAME."

THE PURSUIT.

WHITE GHOST.

As the ship of the desert had turned around under Tim's able guidance, and came hurrying back, it, too, passed between the great pillars of sand, without coming to grief.   Up to the boy dashed the machine, and Jack boarded her.

# A FLIGHT DOWN UNDER

IN SEPTEMBER 1900, Archie Campion cabled Frank Reade Jr. from China with welcome news and a special request: "SAFE IN PEKING WITH LILY AND BOILERPLATE. LACKING TRANSPORTATION. CAN YOU LEND WINGS?"

Archie and his mechanical man had succeeded in rescuing Lily Campion, Archie's sister, from the Boxer Rebellion—but they were in need of an airlift. Frank Jr. replied: "WILL DEPART AT ONCE, ON CONDITION THAT YOU NEXT ACCOMPANY US TO AUSTRALIA FOR THE CHRISTENING OF A NATION."

> This issue dramatized the Reades' rescue of Archie and Lily Campion after the Boxer Rebellion in China.

Frank Jr. immediately started prepping his airship *Cloud Sprite* to leave for China. When Kate, who adored Lily Campion, found out why, she insisted on going with him.

◆ *Poor Lily! Imagine what she endured, being under siege for months, fighting off ferocious attacks by the Chinese, never knowing if help would arrive too late! Papa won't have the faintest notion of what to say or do around her. I told him he must let me come aboard as copilot and organizer of the Women's Committee.*

KATE READE, LETTER TO FRANK READE III
(SEPTEMBER 21, 1900)

On October 3, the *Cloud Sprite* touched down in Peking (now Beijing) to collect the Campions and Boilerplate, then spirited them away to Australia. The rest of the Reade family met them in Sydney to ring in the new year and, with it, the new Australian Commonwealth. "Never was a moonlit midnight in Sydney marked by a wilder, more prolonged, or generally discordant welcome than was December 31, 1900," wrote Alfred Deakin, Australia's second prime minister, in the London *Morning Post.*

On January 1, 1901, the six British colonies that made up Australia were united into one country. Frank Jr. headed an American delegation that had built a ceremonial arch, one of many erected for the inauguration of the Commonwealth. The Reades, Campions, and Boilerplate took part in a celebratory parade through Sydney, with an audience of half a million people. Every roadside, window, balcony, and rooftop along the parade route was packed with cheering spectators.

◆ *Guns boomed and bells chimed to signal the starting of the procession. The long-expected pageant moved in stately majesty along its appointed course, and the bright rays of the sun beating upon the brilliant uniforms of the soldiery presented a picture of unsurpassed*

Kate Reade dresses the part during her trip to the Australian outback. Kate and Lily Campion were impressed by the fact that two states in the new nation gave voting rights to female citizens. Women in the United States wouldn't get the vote until 1920, and Australian Aborigines would have to wait sixty years.

FRANK READE WEEKLY MAGAZINE,
Containing Stories of Adventures on Land, Sea & in the Air.

Issued Weekly—By Subscription $2.50 per year. Application made for Second-Class Entry at N. Y. Post Office.

No. 64.    NEW YORK, JANUARY 15, 1904.    Price 5 Cents.

OVER TWO CONTINENTS; —(OR)— FRANK READE, JR'S LONG DISTANCE FLIGHT. By "NONAME"

The Mongols now began to press furiously toward them. It became a question if their ammunition would hold out. They had three cartridges each when the airship was one hundred yards over the top of the pagoda.

*magnificence. The tramp of horses and marching men resounded along the wood-blocked streets, echoed by the metallic foot-steps of Professor Campion's Mechanical Marvel in the American procession.*

THE INAUGURAL CELEBRATIONS OF THE COMMONWEALTH OF AUSTRALIA (GOVERNMENT PRINTER, 1904)

The Reades and Campions spent the next few months exploring the country, in a rare respite from their often hectic lives.

◆ *We all had such jolly times in Australia, it would have been lovely to stay on there. Do you know, the girls here at Bryn Mawr refuse to believe my tales about the aboriginals and kangaroos and suffragists! You simply must come visit and convince them.*

KATE READE, LETTER TO LILY CAMPION (OCTOBER 13, 1902)

☆☆

Frank Jr., Archie Campion, and Archie's robot Boilerplate stand under the ceremonial American Arch in Sydney. Sponsored by Frank Jr., it was built to celebrate the inauguration of the Commonwealth of Australia in 1901.

# GUNBOATS and DOLLARS

**F**RANK READE JR. and Archie Campion remained lifelong friends, even though they were constantly arguing about social and political issues. Some of their hottest debates were sparked by U.S. military intervention in other nations.

◆ *You fail to recognize that these backwater nations do not understand how to govern themselves or manage business. They are eternally in debt, despite their bounty of natural resources, and eternally in rebellion. To protect the hallowed borders of our nation, we must protect our neighbors against their own bungling as well as against encroachment by other Great Powers.*

FRANK READE JR., LETTER TO ARCHIBALD CAMPION
(DECEMBER 17, 1906)

For three decades, from 1885 through 1916, Frank Jr. helped wage an undeclared war on Latin America. While working as a contractor for the United States Office of Naval Intelligence (ONI), he took part in a dozen military actions. His submarines sank ships in Venezuela and Cuba; his airships laid down cover fire for U.S. Marines in Haiti, Mexico, Nicaragua, and the Dominican Republic; and his electric land rovers smashed through rebel lines in all those countries, plus Honduras and Panama.

## — "IN SEARCH OF MONSTERS" —

**A**CCORDING TO official records, the U.S. Navy sent armed forces to the Central America/Caribbean region more than forty times between 1885 and 1926. The reason most often cited is "to protect American interests."

Technically speaking, these actions weren't wars. Teddy Roosevelt called them "the exercise of an international police power." Frank Jr., like many men of his era, saw them as another opportunity for adventure and profit. Archie didn't share their view of the situation.

◆ *I respectfully suggest that you reconsider your strategy for the national defense. There is but little distinction between policing an entire hemisphere and imperial conquest. It is impossible to sustain both an empire abroad and a democratic republic at home. In the eloquent words of J. Q. Adams, America "goes not abroad in search of monsters to destroy," and "her glory is not dominion, but liberty."*

ARCHIBALD CAMPION, LETTER TO FRANK READE JR.
(JANUARY 6, 1907)

Frank Jr. thought Archie's actions were inconsistent with his lofty words.

◆ *Sir, your suggestion seems at odds with your invention of a mechanical soldier. And, if memory serves, with your volunteering to assist the United States military intervention in China in order that you could rescue Lily. There is no sense in favoring one war but not another; war is war, and always for the same reasons. The best strategy is to be on the winning side. In answer to Mr. Adams—when I serve my country, I serve always as an agent of liberty.*

FRANK READE JR., LETTER TO ARCHIBALD CAMPION
(FEBRUARY 2, 1907)

Teddy Roosevelt sports his Rough Riders uniform as he patrols the Caribbean in this political cartoon.

Studio portraits of Frank Reade Jr., taken around the beginning and end of his participation in the Banana Wars.

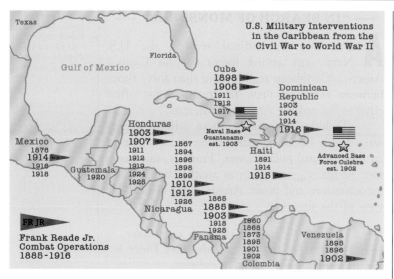

U.S. Military Interventions in the Caribbean from the Civil War to World War II

Frank Reade Jr. Combat Operations 1885-1916

The Banana Wars is an umbrella term for the U.S. military's many interventions in Caribbean nations to protect American business interests.

Those varied interests included banking and finance, agriculture, mining, railroads, telegraph lines, and strategic control of the Panama Canal. The phrase can be traced back to author O. Henry's description of Honduras, where the United Fruit Company controlled all banana exports and related railways and real estate, as a "banana republic."

For decades, whenever Hondurans challenged foreign dominance over their government and economy, the corporation would call in the marines.

Frank Jr. on a mission with his sub *Brizo*. Mercenaries, or "private contractors" as they're called today, have a long history with the military worldwide. They are often paid more than a nation's own soldiers and are not required to comply with military codes of conduct or chains of command. The U.S. Department of Defense currently spends more than $100 billion per year on private military services.

## — GOVERNMENT MAN —

FRANK JR. preferred to work as a contractor, instead of selling his vehicles and weapons to the government, to maintain control over his technology. The U.S. military was glad to hire him for the same reasons it uses private contractors in the twenty-first century: business connections and plausible deniability.

Frank Jr.'s government service was a frequent subject of dime-novel plots, but the truth about his missions was kept out of print.

## — PANAMANIAN REVOLT —
### Colombia 1885

IN 1885, Panama was still part of Colombia. Frank Jr.'s first mission for the newly formed ONI was to suppress a Panamanian rebellion that had destroyed the U.S. consulate in Colón. Serving with Commander Bowman H. McCalla, Frank Jr. used the *Valiant's* electric weapons to help the U.S. Navy take Colón, then Panama City.

➤ *The preparations of Captain McCalla for taking possession of the city of Panama were so thorough and so secret that when, at 3 o'clock yesterday, the order was given for the men to turn out under arms, no one but the officers who were to command columns knew of the intended occupation of the town . . . There were no sounds of drums or bugles, only a solid, steady tramp, tramp, and the glittering of the sun on the helmets and bayonets of the marines.*

*The splendid manner in which the troops entered the city, accompanied by a novel electric battle-wagon, excited the admiration of all who saw it. "Ah!" exclaimed the captain of an English man-of-war in the harbor when he heard of it, "I know those marines. I saw them at Alexandria."*

"THE OCCUPATION OF PANAMA," *NEW YORK TRIBUNE* (MAY 8, 1885)

The invasion of Panama City violated U.S. President Grover Cleveland's policy of minimum involvement in "the political or social disorders of Colombia." American forces were withdrawn from Panama City on the same day they marched in. Nevertheless, the situation generated a lot of press coverage that helped make the case for building up the U.S. Navy. It also set the stage for future interventions by the Marines and Frank Reade Jr.

## — OPERATION: FALSE FLAG —
### Cuba 1898

ONE DIME-NOVEL STORY accidentally came so close to revealing an actual covert operation that the U.S. government brought in author Luis Senarens for questioning. Titled "Six Days Under Havana Harbor; or, Frank Reade, Jr.'s Secret Service Work for Uncle Sam" (*Frank Reade Library* #183), it depicts Frank Jr. using his submarine the *Filibuster* to spy on Spanish naval defenses in Cuba.

During the buildup to the Spanish-American War, Assistant Secretary of the U.S. Navy Theodore Roosevelt had, in fact, sent Frank Jr. to secretly patrol Cuban waters in his submarine *Neptune* and report on the Spanish navy's activities. That's where the resemblance to Senarens's story ends.

The battleship USS *Maine* exploded in Havana Harbor while Frank Jr. was there, giving expansionist factions in the United States an excuse to invade Cuba. At the time, the sinking was blamed on a Spanish mine or torpedo. Frank Jr.'s journal implies that he may have fired the fatal volley from the *Neptune*.

➤ *It is a hard truth that in order to protect our nation's sphere of influence, sacrifices must be made and actions must be taken that would be unpardonable under other conditions. The* Maine *is a case in point, though the explosion of the ship's ammunition magazine is a regrettable piece of ill fortune. Her sacrifice of 266 souls was greater than necessary.*

JOURNAL OF FRANK READE JR. (FEBRUARY 15, 1898)

Crew members aboard a Reade-works submarine. Frank Jr. is standing at the very back of the contingent.

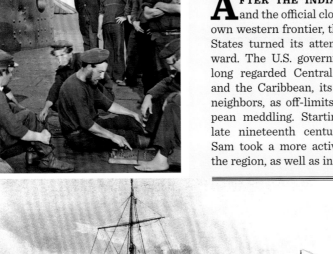

The USS *Maine* prior to her destruction. Recently discovered evidence hints that Asst. Secretary of the Navy Theodore Roosevelt ordered the *Maine* to be secretly sunk by Frank Reade Jr. to trigger the Spanish-American War.

# THE
# ROOSEVELT
## COROLLARY

**A**FTER THE INDIAN WARS and the official closing of its own western frontier, the United States turned its attention outward. The U.S. government had long regarded Central America and the Caribbean, its southern neighbors, as off-limits to European meddling. Starting in the late nineteenth century, Uncle Sam took a more active role in the region, as well as in Asia.

*If a nation shows that it knows how to act with reasonable efficiency and decency in social and political matters, if it keeps order and pays its obligations, it need fear no interference from the United States . . .*

*In asserting the Monroe Doctrine, in taking such steps as we have taken in regard to Cuba, Venezuela, and Panama, and in endeavoring to circumscribe the theater of war in the Far East, and to secure the open door in China, we have acted in our own interest as well as in the interest of humanity at large.*

THEODORE ROOSEVELT,
ANNUAL MESSAGE TO CONGRESS
(DECEMBER 6, 1904)

This rationale for military action and nation building became known as the Roosevelt Corollary to the Monroe Doctrine. ★★

Admiral Dewey's White Fleet steams toward Venezuela to confront the Imperial German Navy, 1902.

U.S. medal for service in Cuba, 1906.

## — GERMAN-ANGLO BLOCKADE — 
### Venezuela 1902 – 1903

ON FRANK JR.'s next covert submarine operation, his task was to dissuade the German Imperial Navy from taking over Venezuela. Germany and England were blockading Venezuela's main port, trying to force the country into resuming payments on its national debt. The German forces had captured and sunk several vessels.

Theodore Roosevelt, now president, was suspicious of any German incursions as possible first steps in an attack on the United States. Though he didn't know it yet, Germany had drawn up contingency plans to invade America's eastern seaboard.

Teddy ordered fifty-three U.S. battleships to converge on the Caribbean in a show of force.

Venezuela:
*"Better mind your Monroe Doctrine! That German is making trouble."*

Uncle Sam:
*"The Monroe Doctrine will keep you from being kidnapped, sonny; but it won't help you get out of your honest debts."*

When German ships bombarded Fort San Carlos in Venezuela, all-out war with Germany looked likely. To avoid a direct showdown, Roosevelt gave the go-ahead for ONI to send in Frank Jr.

➤ *Papa has gone off to South America—to Venezuela, I think—in one of his submersible ships, at the beck and call of his Navy friends. Something to do with the Germans. I know your father dislikes the Kaiser, but I ask you, what does it matter to us if Wilhelm wants to fuss about down there? At times I wonder if both our fathers will always be big little boys playing soldier.*

KATE READE, LETTER TO ALICE ROOSEVELT
(DECEMBER 12, 1902)

On January 23, 1903, Germany's battleship *Kaiser Wilhelm I* sank, apparently torpedoed, in an incident that has never been publicly acknowledged. The Germans got the message and grudgingly agreed to arbitration with Venezuela. Pulitzer Prize–winning historian Edmund Morris writes that the historical record of the Venezuela Crisis contains "an extraordinary void, hinting at some vanished enormity, in the archives of three nations."

### THE ORIGINAL 
## — BANANA REPUBLIC — 
### Honduras 1903, 1907

TWICE, Frank Jr. saw action in Honduras with U.S. Marines led by Major Smedley Butler. The first time, in March 1903, they drove straight through a firefight between opposing factions to rescue the American consul. They found him "quivering under the floor boards, swaddled in Old Glory," according to Frank Jr.'s journal.

General Manuel Bonilla won the firefight and ruled Honduras until he was ousted in 1907.

During that conflict, U.S. Marines landed at Puerto Cortés to protect America's banana trade. On the other side of the country, Frank Jr. blasted his way through enemy lines, then took the deposed dictator aboard the USS *Chicago*. Bonilla was later reinstated as president, after a 1911 coup financed by the Cuyamel Fruit Company.

### — "HUSH, OR FRANK READE — WILL GET YOU"
### Nicaragua 1912

A POPULAR REVOLT rose up against the U.S.-backed government of Nicaragua in 1912. On August 14, Major Butler and 350 marines, along with Frank Jr. and his armed ATV *Intrepid,* landed at Corinto and made their way to the capital, Managua. Butler took command of the government's army of four thousand men, writing in a letter to his mother, "this move of mine must not become public . . . but it is the only way for this government to win, and the State Department, I surmise, is anxious that it should continue in power."

Smedley Butler's marines signal the flagship USS *California* as it approaches Corinto, Nicaragua, 1912. Painting by legendary Arrow Shirts ad illustrator J. C. Leyendecker.

The *Neptune* takes on provisions in the Orinoco River, Venezuela, 1902. This Readeworks submarine sank the German battleship *Kaiser Wilhelm I* and set the Germans on a course toward U-boat development.

U.S. medal
for service in
Nicaragua,
1912.

U.S. medal for
service in Mexico,
1914.

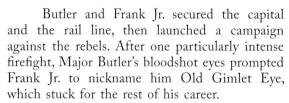

A U.S. soldier
searches a resident
of Veracruz during
the occupation.

U.S. medal for
service in Haiti,
1915.

Butler and Frank Jr. secured the capital and the rail line, then launched a campaign against the rebels. After one particularly intense firefight, Major Butler's bloodshot eyes prompted Frank Jr. to nickname him Old Gimlet Eye, which stuck for the rest of his career.

The fighting ended in a government victory at the Battle of Cayotepe on October 3. "We took the rebel General's surrender in the dead of night," as Frank Jr. describes the scene, "in his stronghold, an old lantern-lit church that was littered with weapons."

Years later, an article in *The Nation* reported that Nicaraguan mothers still warned naughty children to "Hush, or Frank Reade will get you!" The United States occupied the country until 1933.

## — OCCUPATION OF VERACRUZ —
### Mexico 1914

DURING THE CHAOS of the Mexican Revolution, the United States sent warships south to protect American businesses in Mexico. In April 1914, a minor incident involving U.S. sailors escalated into major tension between the two nations. When U.S. President Woodrow Wilson got word that a big arms shipment was bound for Veracruz, he ordered the U.S. Navy to intercept it and occupy the city.

ONI at once dispatched Frank Reade Jr. with Major Smedley Butler. Frank Jr. rained down electric gunfire from his helicopter ship the *Eagle*, covering Butler and his marines while

they went from house to house, pacifying opposition. With additional backup from Pompei in the *Valiant*, they took most of Veracruz in only two days.

Resistance from the Mexican populace was so fierce, however, that Wilson scrapped Butler's plan to capture Mexico City. That was Frank Jr.'s cue to leave. "Military occupation is dangerous yet dull," his journal comments. "I would rather die in combat than be bored to death."

## — NATION BUILDING —
### Haiti 1915

HAITI, a former plantation colony of France, rebelled against its slave masters and gained independence in 1804. Forced to pay reparations to France, the new nation went deep into debt.

By 1915, when Frank Jr. and Smedley Butler arrived on the scene, Haiti's people were mired in poverty, its currency was owned by international bankers, and its latest dictator had just been hacked to pieces in a grisly public spectacle of retribution. On top of that, with Europe at war, the United States was again worried about possible German encroachment.

On July 28, Frank Jr. served as armed backup in the sky while 330 U.S. Marines came ashore at Port-au-Prince "to protect American and foreign lives and property" and "preserve

U.S. Troops
Marching
in Streets of
Vera Cruz.

The *Valiant* in Mexico, 1914.

order." The force soon swelled to two thousand men.

Major Butler and Colonel Littleton Waller led a deadly campaign against Haitian rebels. During their first foray into the interior of Haiti, Waller ordered Frank Jr.'s ATV *Vigilant* to be mounted on a railcar. They battled their way up the line, securing the railroad for transporting U.S. troops and materials. The *Vigilant*'s electrified firepower was so devastating that resistance proved futile.

Maj. Smedley Butler, Sgt. Ross Iams, and Pvt. Samuel Gross depicted taking Fort Rivière, Haiti, on November 17, 1915. Frank Jr. provided close air support with his helicopter *Eagle* during this battle.

Frank Reade Jr.'s *Eagle* acts as aerial support for the USS *Washington*, Twelfth Company of Marines, during the invasion of Haiti on July 28, 1915.

# SEND IN THE MARINE

**F**RANK READE JR.'S career as a military contractor brought him into contact with the same officers in many different battles—notably Colonel Littleton Waller, whom he'd met in Egypt in 1882, and Marine Major Smedley Butler, a pivotal figure in the Banana Wars. Because Marines could be portrayed as a temporary peacekeeping force, not an invading army, they were often deployed to protect American interests.

Butler, who reached the rank of Major General, is the U.S. military's most highly decorated marine. He saw combat in the Philippines, China, the Caribbean, Central America, and World War I, fighting alongside Boilerplate as well as Frank Reade Jr. Butler remains the only person to be awarded the Brevet Medal and two Medals of Honor, each for a different combat action.

Butler's military accomplishments should have enshrined him in American history, but his post-military pursuits earned him obscurity instead. Initially gung ho for battle, he grew resentful of the U.S. military being used

as a "thug for Big Business." Nonetheless, he did his duty exceedingly well and kept his mouth shut in public while he was in active service.

After Butler retired, he finally felt free to voice the opinions formed during his service. The decorated war hero became an outspoken critic of U.S. military adventurism and war profiteering. He spoke to church and veterans' groups, donating his fees to charity. In his speeches and in print, Butler explained the workings of what U.S. President (and former general) Dwight Eisenhower later called the "military-industrial complex."

◆ *I spent 33 years and four months in active military service and during that period I spent most of my time as a high class thug for Big Business, for Wall Street and the bankers. In short, I was a racketeer, a gangster for capitalism.*

*I helped make Mexico and especially Tampico safe for American oil interests in 1914. I helped make Haiti and Cuba a decent place for the National City Bank boys to collect revenues in. I helped in the raping of half a dozen Central American republics for the benefit of Wall Street. I helped purify Nicaragua for the International Banking House of Brown Brothers in 1902–1912. I brought light to the Dominican Republic for the American sugar interests in 1916. I helped make Honduras right for the American fruit companies in 1903. In China in 1927 I helped see to it that Standard Oil went on its way unmolested.*

*Looking back on it, I might have given Al Capone a few hints. The best he could do was to operate his racket in three districts. I operated on three continents.*

MAJOR GENERAL SMEDLEY D. BUTLER, *WAR IS A RACKET* (ROUND TABLE PRESS, 1935)

★★

Frank Reade Jr. and Electric Bob in the airship *Eagle,* which was flown on several missions in the Banana Wars.

U.S. medal for service in the Dominican Republic, 1916.

◆ *Finally, the Haitian rebels are broken. They made their last stand at Fort Rivière, an old French bastion atop a mountain at 4,000 feet. Our bombardment from the* Eagle *kept them pinned down, while Maj. Butler and his men finished off the desperate defenders in hand-to-hand combat.*

*Pomp's reaction, and his general behavior on this expedition, have been strangely subdued, but he will not say why. His usual exuberance is sorely missed.*

JOURNAL OF FRANK READE JR. (NOVEMBER 19, 1915)

Haiti was occupied by the United States until 1934. Pompei continued to work with the Reades into the 1920s, but he never went on another ONI mission with Frank Jr.

## — MOPPING UP —

LESS THAN SIX MONTHS after leaving Haiti, Frank Jr. was sent to the Dominican Republic to put down yet another revolution. "These countries, these wars, are all beginning to blur together," he lamented. "I need a fresh challenge." It was his final operation in the Caribbean.

Kate Reade was working for ONI years later, when she pieced together the facts of these missions from her father's journal and other sources.

◆ *I knew Papa did jobs for the Navy, but I had no idea how many. Funny, I followed in his footsteps without even knowing where they were.*

JOURNAL OF KATE READE (AUGUST 9, 1934)

☆☆

# CENTRAL and SOUTH AMERICAN ADVENTURES

ASTRAY IN THE SELVAS!

OR, THE WILD EXPERIENCES OF FRANK READE, JR. —IN— SOUTH AMERICA

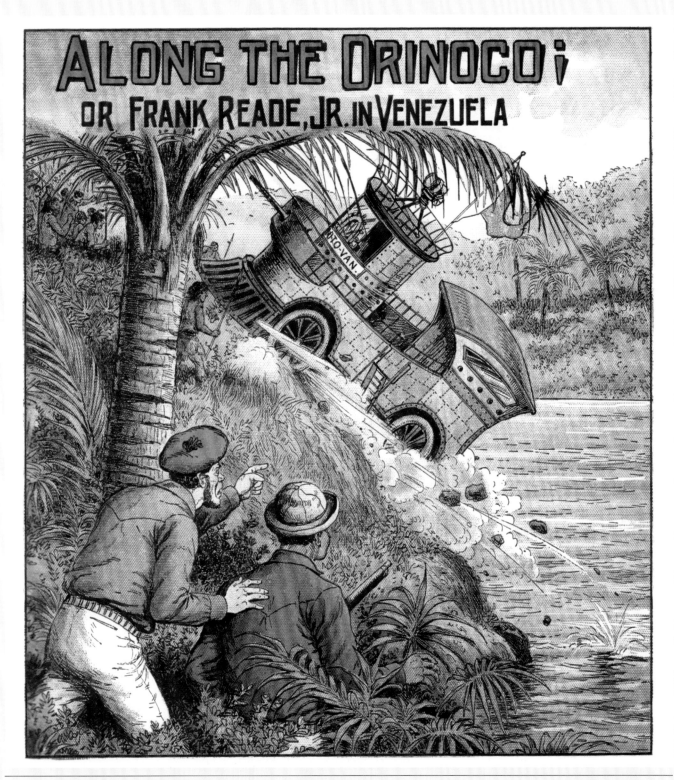

**Frank Reade Jr. IN CUBA**
— or —
**HELPING THE PATRIOTS WITH HIS**
**LATEST AIRSHIP**
*Frank Reade Library #159*

## CHAPTER II
### *Over Cuba*

The air-ship's rate of speed increased to fifty-five miles an hour and the *Jupiter* fairly skimmed over the ocean, with a long drag rope hanging down having a grapnel on the end.

The spy silently watched Barney manipulating the wheel and the levers, and noted the fact that each room was well supplied with various kinds of weapons of warfare.

"You seem to have her well armed," said Blanco to Frank at noontime, as they went out on one of the side platforms.

"Oh, yes—we have started out for war and had to be prepared," answered the inventor, carelessly. "Did you notice the small trap doors in the floors? They cover compartments filled with petards. If we hovered over a Spanish army of fifty thousand men and began to drop those shells down from the sky upon them, in a very short space of time we would annihilate them."

When the Spaniard went inside and saw the shells under the traps, he made up his mind to destroy the *Jupiter* with them. An evil plan had entered his scheming mind, and he made secret preparations to carry it out. Frank had no idea of the villainy resident in the man's mind.

Blanco crept silently into one of the rooms, opened a trap door, and lit the fuse of a bomb with a match. "It will burst in five minutes," he chuckled, "and blow his dangerous craft and crew to perdition!"

Closing the trap, he hastened out on one of the side platforms, seized the drag rope and slid down to the grapnel on the end. It was too high from the ground for him to drop off yet, so he waited there for a favorable opportunity to occur.

## CHAPTER IV
### *The Burst Shell*

The shell Blanco had ignited suddenly exploded! The fearful shock hurled the *Jupiter* high in the air, tore the floor of the middle room to pieces, destroyed most of the contents of the apartment, and ripped several gaping holes in the roof. Frank and his companions were thrown down.

Most of the flying fragments of the shell went downward, and drove the rest of the petards toward the ground in a heavy shower. The explosion had rent several of the electric wires, cutting the circuit, and as the *Jupiter*'s mechanism stopped, she ceased rolling and swaying, and darted earthward again, with a swift gliding motion.

Frank, half dazed, bounded to his feet. "Good heavens, what was that explosion?" he asked. The young inventor flung open the door, and was going to dash into the next room when he saw that most of the floor was gone.

He recoiled, and looked startled, for the wonder was that the car did not part entirely in two from the explosion. "Blanco!" he shouted. **FR**

# THE SILENT SERVICE

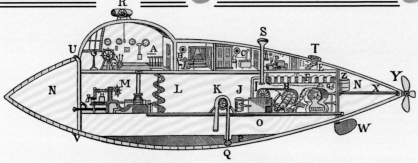

EXPLANATION OF ILLUSTRATION

A—Pilot-house.
B—State room.
C—Kitchen.
D—Store room.
E—Exit chamber.
F—Storage batteries.
G—Electric motor.
H—Dynamo.
I—Oil engine.
J—Oil tank.
K—Water pump.
L—Companionway.
M—Air engine.

N—Air chamber.
O—Water reservoir.
P—Lead ballast.
Q—Water valve.
R—Search-light.
S—Engine funnel.
T—Trap door.
U—Air valve.
V—Escape valve.
W—Rudder.
X—Shaft.
Y—Screw.
Z—Chemical tank.

*Popular Science* magazine ran this speculative diagram of a Readeworks submarine in the 1880s.

The *Brizo* breaches the sea's surface.

WHEN JULES VERNE'S *20,000 Leagues Under the Sea* was published in 1869, the submarine had been in existence for nearly a century. In both the American Revolution and the War of 1812, Americans built submersible vessels to fight the British navy. These early efforts proved that underwater warfare was possible, but they failed to sink any English ships. The first sinking of a warship by a submarine was during the American Civil War, when the Confederate sub CSS *Hunley* sank the USS *Housatonic*.

In the 1880s, the Spanish and German navies developed electric subs, but their range was so limited by battery power that they were effectively useless. The Reades, ahead of the game, had already invented their own nickel-cadmium batteries. Their subs were far more practical and more technologically advanced than anything else on or under the sea.

Around the turn of the century, the U.S. Navy commissioned its first sub, the USS *Holland*. Russia, Japan, and England followed suit, beginning a new era in naval combat.

Germany jump-started its submarine research after Frank Reade Jr. used a Readeworks sub to sink the battleship *Kaiser Wilhelm I* in the 1902 Venezuela Crisis. When World War I began, Germany was at the forefront of the undersea arms race, with a new generation of submersible called an *Unterseeboot*, or "U-boat." ★ ★

Frank Jr.'s successful use of the submarine as a weapon inspired Germany to start developing U-boats at the beginning of the twentieth century. The most infamous result was the German submarine U-20 torpedoing the passenger liner RMS *Lusitania* in 1915.

# UNDERSEA ADVENTURES

*Master special-effects artist Ray Harryhausen was inspired by this Frank Reade story to include a sunken city and a fight with a giant crab in his film adaptation of Jules Verne's* Mysterious Island. *These elements aren't in the original Verne novel.*

FRANK READE, JR's ELECTRIC SEA ENGINE;
OR, HUNTING FOR A SUNKEN DIAMOND MINE.

THE UNDERGROUND SEA;
OR, FRANK READE, JR's SUBTERRANEAN CRUISE.

Frank Reade Jr. EXPLORING A
## SUBMARINE MOUNTAIN
— or —
## LOST
### AT THE BOTTOM OF THE SEA
*Frank Reade Library #77*

Down the street of the sunken city the explorers walked. They came to a broad, paved square, fully two acres in extent. On all sides rose high, templelike structures.

To Frank there occurred many startling thoughts. How many centuries had elapsed since these streets were thronged with an intelligent people, or these silent houses inhabited! It was a wonderful thing to contemplate and made a deep impression on all. That the former inhabitants of the sunken city had been no ordinary people, there was little doubt. The extent of their city, the architecture of their houses was all evidence that they were to a high degree civilized.

But one and all, with their unknown manners and customs, their speech and their personality, they had passed away. The sea had swallowed them up. Their fate was only one of its many mighty and strange secrets.

Suddenly Barney gave a leap toward Frank, waving his arms in alarm. Down the street there came a strange sea monster. It was of the crab species, but had longer legs, was capable of great speed, and had a tremendous beak and fierce eyes. It was of giant size, and its yellow armor glittered in the electric light most strangely.

Straight for the three divers it came. That it regarded them as its prey seemed certain.

At once the divers started in retreat. But the sea monster could take three strides in their one, and gained upon them every moment.

Frank, glancing over his shoulder, saw that they were certain to be over-taken. The crab was not fifty yards in their rear. The submarine *Tortoise* was a quarter of a mile away.

So Frank, who was in advance, set the example for the others by darting into a doorway. Barney and Pomp followed him. They were in a small building, but the crab could not pursue them further, for its body was too large to get in the door. It took up a position at the door, and seemed disposed to

*No nineteenth-century nautical adventure would be complete without an attack by a cephalopod.*

wait patiently until its prey should come out.

Here was indeed a situation. The divers were now in a quandary. How were they to get back to the submarine boat?

Frank Reade, Jr., was not to be baffled. His inventive genius soon hit upon a plan. Placing his helmet close to Pomp's, he shouted: "We must make our way back over the roofs!"

The house tops were flat after the ancient fashion. Once upon the roof it was easy work to cross from one to another. This was done, and the party were making rapid progress when suddenly a strange movement of the water caused them to look back.

The crab in some manner divined their purpose and was coming again in close pursuit. They were not as yet half way to the *Tortoise*. Frank thought of again seeking refuge in some building, but before a roof trap could be found the crab was upon them.

One of its claws seized Barney by the leg. The Celt fell and went under the monster. It seemed at that moment as if the brave Irishman's fate was sealed. But he made a savage blow at his foe with his knife. It struck the crab in the lower part of its jaw and sent a stream of milky liquid out into the water. In a moment the water was so clouded with this that not one in the party could see a foot in any direction.

Frank and Pomp were the next moment also in the crab's clutches. Then followed a fight such as none of them ever forgot. It was deadly and desperate. It was a battle in the dark, literally speaking. Its perils were multifarious. For the puncturing of the air reservoir or the helmets of the diving suits meant death to the divers.

All they could do was strike out at random. But Frank succeeded in severing one of the crab's claws with a blow of his ax. Barney was underneath, thrusting right and left with his knife. And it was left for him to strike the death blow. By a stroke of luck he reached a vital part of the crab's anatomy. The monster reeled and fell over dead. **FR**

# FRANK READE

## WEEKLY MAGAZINE,

### Containing Stories of Adventures on Land, Sea & in the Air.

*Issued Weekly—By Subscription $2.50 per year. Application made for Second-Class Entry at N. Y. Post Office.*

No. 62.   NEW YORK, JANUARY 1, 1904.   Price 5 Cents.

# LOST IN THE GREAT UNDERTOW;

## OR, FRANK READE, JR.'S SUBMARINE CRUISE IN THE GULF STREAM.

### BY "NONAME."

At that moment the professor and Pomp saw the submarine boat. They had been victims of an awful
despair. They made excited gestures. But Frank was drawing the Octopus
as near the wreck as possible.

# FRANK READE

## WEEKLY MAGAZINE,

### Containing Stories of Adventures on Land, Sea & in the Air.

*Issued Weekly—By Subscription $2.50 per year. Entered as Second Class Matter at the New York Post Office, 1902, by Frank Tousey.*

No. 8.     NEW YORK, DECEMBER 19, 1902.     Price 5 Cents.

# FRANK READE, JR'S DEEP SEA DIVER THE "TORTOISE;" OR, THE SEARCH FOR A SUNKEN ISLAND.
## By "NONAME."

Through the obscured water there came a powerful set of long, sinuous arms, which almost instantly enfolded Frank Reade, Jr. The young inventor was, like a flash, swept away
and out of sight. Barney stood like one overcome with awful horror.

# 4
# AGE OF
# YOUTH

THE NEXT GENERATION OF READES—Kate and Frank III—came of age in a whole new world. Amazing nineteenth-century inventions such as electric lights and telephones were becoming a familiar, even necessary, part of twentieth-century life for many people. With each passing year, the frontiers of science moved farther away from the simple steam engines that had launched Readeworks. Kate and her brother took different paths in search of new frontiers.

Like the generations before them, Kate Reade and Frank III got the dime-novel treatment. In this adventure, they team up with Pompei's son, Scipio, and Barney's son, Larry.

## EARLY BIRD

AFTER THE READE FAMILY got home from Australia in 1901, Frank Jr. again stuck around for a while to work on new vehicle designs. To everyone's surprise, his son started tinkering alongside him for the first time. Although Frank Reade III and his grandpa got on well with each other and collaborated on several engineering projects, they both had a hard time relating to Frank Jr.

Frank III's vehicles were much smaller and more modern-looking than his father's. His early efforts included a compact, highly maneuverable submarine and an armored car. Frank Jr., who loved to build airships the size of today's jet airliners, found his son's designs intriguing but lacking in grandeur. "Frankie builds first-rate machines," he wrote in 1901, "but he does not 'think big.'"

Huge helicopter airships were no big deal to Frank III, since he had grown up in and

Frank III's newly constructed sub is launched at Lake Reade, a lake built next to Readeworks for testing nautical vehicles.

around them. More thrilling to him was the sensation of flying a one-man set of wings, which he likened to "dancing in the air."

As a teen, he'd been inspired to build gliders after meeting aviation pioneers Otto "Glider King" Lilienthal and Samuel P. Langley. Frank III's designs were way ahead of their time, with advantages no one else would discover for decades, such as a horizontal pilot.

Sketches by Frank III for one of his gliders.

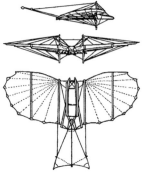

◆ *You should see our little Frankie fly, riding the wind on his wings! I am enclosing one of his clever drawings. A kind word from you about it, if you are so inclined, would mean the world to him.*

EMILIE READE, LETTER TO FRANK READE JR. (MARCH 8, 1896)

## — RACE TO FLIGHT —

AROUND THE TURN of the century, while Frank Jr. ruled the skies in his flying boats, the race to design a motor-driven, fixed-wing airplane exploded into a worldwide obsession. Aviators and inventors everywhere, including Frank III, chased the eternal dream of soaring like a bird.

The Readeworks dual-battery electrical system was too heavy for small aircraft, so Frankie teamed up with V-8 motorcycle racer Glenn Curtiss—the "fastest man on earth"—to build a

The Reade family's unique way of windsailing, as witnessed by a conventional balloonist. The Reades enjoyed outings in these paragliders, but they were impractical for long-distance travel.

new internal combustion engine. Curtiss and Frank III contributed key innovations as members of Alexander Graham Bell's Aerial Experiment Association (AEA). Frank Jr. had mixed feelings about his son's aviation career.

◆ *I am gratified that Frankie shows strong interest in aeronautics, yet disappointed in his adoption of the gasoline engine. It is inefficient, noisy, and noxious. Electricity remains the superior motive power.*

*Moreover, Frankie does not consider putting his inventions to practical use. What good is flying for its own sake, without a destination? His aeroplane would be well suited for military application such as inconspicuous aerial reconnaissance and precise bombardment.*

JOURNAL OF FRANK READE JR. (AUGUST 11, 1908)

Frank III rescues survivors of a shipwreck.

Unlike Frank Jr., Kate Reade was enthralled by flight in every form. She loved flying airplanes and airships alike.

◆ *Today I took Frankie's Yellow Bird out for a spin and managed a barrel roll, my first one! For a minute I thought I wouldn't make it—my brains felt as if they wanted to fly straight out of my head. Then all at once the ground and sky were revolving around me and I felt perfectly beautiful, swooping and diving like a swallow.*

KATE READE, LETTER TO TEXAS GUINAN (SEPTEMBER 1, 1908)

Frank III at the bow of his submarine during trials in Delaware Bay. Electric Bob and Barney O'Shea can be seen at the conning tower at right.

Frank Reade III prepares to test his armored car in downtown Readestown.

Kate at
the controls of
Frank III's
*Yellow Bird.*

## SKY RIDER

**M**UCH TO HIS father's chagrin, Frank III turned out to love flying more than inventing and showed no interest in covert military operations. After the AEA disbanded, the young pilot helped organize public air shows across the United States and flew in many of them, inspiring the next wave of aviators.

Airplanes were still so new that most people didn't believe they could really fly until they saw it with their own eyes. At the 1910 Los Angeles International Aviation Meet, the first in the nation, Frank III blew away the skeptics when he flew higher than any human being had ever gone.

◆ *Frank Reade III, the daring scion of the Readeworks dynasty, made many thrilling and spectacular flights and proved to be the idol of the meet. He captured the record for height by reaching an altitude of over 4,000 feet. His flight was not only spectacular but it was also a practical demonstration of the fact that the aeroplane is no toy.*
"THE PROGRESS OF THE WORLD—THE LOS ANGELES AVIATION MEET," *THE AMERICAN REVIEW OF REVIEWS* (FEBRUARY 1910)

At the same air show, he met a young woman named Birte Svensson, who boldly asked him to give her flying lessons. Frankie immediately nicknamed her Birdie and started making plans for their future together.

◆ *Thanks to you and sis for coming to cheer me on at the air meet. What grand fun—everyone should have the chance to fly. And I'm ever so glad that you like Birdie, because I'm going to marry that girl. She's a peach!*
FRANK READE III, LETTER TO EMILIE READE (JANUARY 22, 1910)

# PATENT WARS

**G**LENN CURTISS was a pioneer of American aviation. He and Frank Reade III helped develop ailerons (wing flaps) for maneuvering, wheeled landing gear for safety, and dihedral (slanting up) wings for stability—innovations that are standard features on airplanes today. Orville and Wilbur Wright's method of steering the Wright Flyers, by warping the entire wing, was a technological dead end.

Curtiss and Frank III, along with John McCurdy, Frederick "Casey" Baldwin, and U.S. Army lieutenant Thomas Selfridge, were part of the Aerial Experiment Association (AEA) financed by Alexander Graham Bell's wife, Mabel. The Wright brothers declined to join the AEA, which Bell described as a "cooperative scientific association, not for gain but for the love of the art and doing what we can to help one another." Like Frank Jr., the Wrights were secretive about their inventions.

◆ *We have always thought that our best market would be with the governments . . . We have a patent on our early gliding machine, but have not applied for protection on any of our work of the past five years. Reade's exemplar confirms that secrets are worth more to governments than patented articles. For that reason we have taken out no patents since we found there was any practical use in our invention.*
WILBUR WRIGHT, LETTER TO REGINALD FESSENDEN (APRIL 13, 1907)

Their faith in the value of secrecy didn't stop the brothers from demanding royalties and slapping competitors with lawsuits based on that one patent. They argued that their patent encompassed the *concept* of ailerons, even if their airplanes didn't actually have ailerons. The Wrights' aggressive litigation stalled aviation development for nearly a decade. Curtiss, who inherited the AEA's patent on ailerons and founded his own aviation company, was one of their prime targets.

◆ *Sorry to hear those Wright boys are still badgering you. Maybe my Pop's got the right idea about secrecy after all. Readeworks is beyond the reach of the Navy's lawyers and the Wrights', because we never filed patents or sold airships. No royalties for us, but no ugly lawsuits either.*
FRANK READE III, LETTER TO GLENN CURTISS (JANUARY 29, 1912)

It took America's entry into World War I for the U.S. government to end the squabble so that warplanes could be manufactured. Assistant Secretary of the Navy Franklin D. Roosevelt pressured aircraft manufacturers into forming a jointly owned patent pool, partially fulfilling Bell's vision of the AEA. Ironically, the two biggest litigants later merged, forming the Curtiss-Wright Corporation, which is still in operation. ★★

Birte "Birdie" Svensson married Frank III in 1910.

Frank III at the first air show in the United States, the 1910 Los Angeles International Aviation Meet.

Sure enough, Frankie and Birte were married later that year, just before the International Aeronautic Tournament in St. Louis. That show marked one of Frank III's proudest moments as a civilian pilot, when he took a special passenger aloft: Archie Campion's good friend Teddy Roosevelt, in the first airplane flight by a U.S. president.

➤ *We were up about 150 feet, when I felt the machine wiggle a little, and turning around I saw Roosevelt was waving his hat at the crowd in the pavilion seats. The noise from the propeller was so terrific I had to yell with all my lungs, "Be careful, Colonel: don't pull any of those strings." The valve cord was directly over his hand, and the engine would have stopped had he pulled it a little.*

*When we landed safely I felt as though some one had cut off the high pressure on my heart valve . . . He reached over and said, "Frankie, you're all right. It certainly was the biggest day of my life."*

"Reade Story of Flight; Feared He Would Never 'Square' Himself if Roosevelt Should Fall," *New York Times* (October 12, 1910)

☆☆

FIRST IN AMERICA
AVIATION MEET
LOS ANGELES
JANUARY 10-20 1910
American & Foreign Aviators
DAILY FLIGHTS

Former president
Theodore Roosevelt
becomes the first
U.S. president to
fly in an airplane,
courtesy of
Frank Reade III.

# WHO WAS

# FIRST?

**T**HE FAMOUS twelve-second hop of the Wright brothers' motorized glider in 1903 may not have been the first time a human being achieved controlled flight in a powered aircraft. Earlier claimants to the "first in flight" title include Clément Ader (1897) and Augustus Herring (1898).

Gustave Whitehead claimed that he flew a steam-powered monoplane about half a mile in 1899 but crashed into a building. In 1901, newspapers reported that he flew his No. 21 plane more than 2,600 feet at a 50-foot altitude, taking off and landing on wheels from a flat surface at Fairfield, Connecticut. His 1901 flight was a greater achievement than the Wrights' launching their craft from a rail, flying 120 feet at a 10-foot altitude, then landing on skids. Financial and health problems put an end to Whitehead's

work, while the Wrights went on to win military contracts.

First-flight claims were hotly debated, stirring up an intense rivalry between European and American aviators. The U.S. press may have been reluctant to tout a German immigrant such as Whitehead (born Weisskopf), who spoke with a thick accent, as America's representative—especially at a time when political friction with Germany was heating up.

The Wrights had the foresight to photograph their experiment and became fiercely protective of their legend. Due to a dispute over credit given to Samuel P. Langley, Orville Wright refused to let the Smithsonian Institution display the *Wright Flyer* and instead loaned it to the London Science Museum. In 1943, the Smithsonian finally agreed to give the Wright brothers sole credit for the first airplane flight in history, in exchange for the right to display their glider. ★★

There is debate about whether the 1903 *Wright Flyer* was really the first powered, fixed-wing aircraft to achieve controlled flight.

# WILD THING

In this *Young Kate Reade* story, Kate rescues her grandparents from a flash flood along the Delaware River.

This illustration accompanied a story about Kate foiling a train robbery.

In one of the weirder *Young Kate Reade* tales, Kate fights off rats that are being controlled by a sort of evil Pied Piper.

"**W**ILD" Kate Reade earned her nickname at Bryn Mawr College. Athletically as well as intellectually gifted, yet impetuous and unconventional, she could ace an exam one day, then scandalize the school by winning a boxing match the next. When Lily Campion introduced her to Teddy Roosevelt's equally brash daughter Alice, Wild Kate and Princess Alice hit it off at once.

Kate practices fencing with Frank Jr. She enjoyed hand-to-hand combat training as "playtime."

In her twenties, Kate befriended another kindred spirit: future movie star and speakeasy owner Texas Guinan, who was then just getting her start in vaudeville. One night Kate took Texas out joyriding in Frank Jr.'s prize electric ATV, the *Valiant,* and wound up foiling a train robbery. "Papa was all a-sputter and couldn't make up his mind whether to be angry or proud or anxious," wrote Kate, "but in the end pride won the battle." This real-life escapade inspired a spate of *Young Kate Reade* dime-novel stories.

➤ *A man holding two guns stepped into the mail car. He was gloved, wore a slouch hat turned down in front and a black mask, and hence all that could be seen was that he was over three feet and less than ten feet tall.*

*Pointing a gun at each of the men, he announced in a menacing tone that the first man who showed his head at a window or door would be shot. The engineer asked if he should climb on the engine, and was answered: "No!— we'll give you the ride of your lives."*

*Then the crew were all thoroughly scared, for they knew that the hold up men had gotten very little for their pains, and that the bandits planned to throw open the throttle and let the engine go where it would. They would have done so in a flash, if it were not for the fortuitous appearance at that moment of Kate Reade in the wonderful Valiant.*

"THE MAIL CAR ROBBERY; OR,
KATE READE AGAINST THE
BLACK MASK,"
*YOUNG KATE READE* #1

★★

Wild Kate Reade engages in a scandalous boxing match.

STEALING OUT

STUDY

EXERCISE

PILLOW FIGHT

THE "RACKETS" AND DIVERSIONS OF "WILD" KATE READE AT BRYN MAWR.

HOW SHE EVADES HER PRECEPTORS AND GOES OFF WITH THE BOYS—THE PRANKS SHE PLAYS AND PLEASURES
SHE ENJOYS INSIDE AND OUTSIDE OF THE COLLEGE PRECINCTS

Kate takes her turn at the controls during a transcontinental adventure, while her grandfather gets some rest.

# CRUISING *with* PRINCESS ALICE

**A**FTER KATE READE graduated from college, Alice Roosevelt invited her on a cruise to exotic Asia: Japan, the Philippines, China, and Korea. Traveling via ocean liner with U.S. Secretary of War William H. Taft, the two spitfires were treated like A-list celebrities and behaved like rock stars. They were still making the papers several years after their 1905 cruise.

➤ *Miss Roosevelt, clad in a scarlet riding habit, with shining boots, flourishing a whip, had burst on horseback upon an entertainment in her honor, given by the Emperor of Korea at the grave of his consort, and had climbed upon a sacred elephant and, sitting astride there, asked Miss Reade, who was along, to snapshot her. This is according to the account of Fraulein*

# TEXAS GUINAN

## 1884 – 1933

Texas Guinan was Hollywood's first female action-movie hero.

**T**EXAS GUINAN was one of the few women who could keep up with Wild Kate Reade. When the two of them went out on the town together, they were sure to wind up in the next day's gossip columns.

Texas started out in vaudeville doing western-themed acts, then went to Hollywood and gained fame as the silver screen's first cowgirl. She played a pistol-packing action hero in movies such as *The Gun Woman* and *The She Wolf.* Texas ranks as the biggest western actress of the silent era and has a star on the Hollywood Walk of Fame.

When the National Prohibition Act went into effect, she went into the speakeasy business in New York, defying tradition by becoming the first female MC in nightclub history. Texas entertained the most famous names of the age

Guinan became the most famous MC of the Prohibition era.

WESTERN UNION

```
CLASS OF SERVICE                                    SYMBOLS
This is a full-rate                          EL=Day Letter
Telegram or Cable-                           NT=Overnight Telegram
gram unless its de-                          LC=Deferred Cable
ferred character is in-                      NLT=Cable Night Letter
dicated by a suitable
symbol above or pre-
ceding the address.                          Ship Radiogram

The filing time shown in the date line on telegrams and day letters is STANDARD TIME at point of origin. Time of receipt is STANDARD TIME at point of destination

FNB165 57 DL=NEWYORK NY 10 NFT

KATE READE =
    CARE READEWORKS =

AM GIVING RATHER UNIQUE PARTY FOR RAYMOND DUNCAN BROTHER
OF THE FAMED ISADORA TOMORROW EVENING BEGINNING AT
MIDNIGHT AT CASTILLIAN GARDEN PELHAM PARKWAY AND WOULD
LOVE TO HAVE YOU PRESENT STOP WILL BE ABLE TO HEAR ME
DISCUSS ANYTHING FROM NIETSCHE TO DANCING STOP THROW AWAY
YOUR PENCILS AND PAPER AND BE MY BEST GUEST =
    TEXAS GUINAN.

THE COMPANY WILL APPRECIATE SUGGESTIONS FROM ITS PATRONS CONCERNING ITS SERVICE
```

One of many telegrams exchanged between Texas Guinan and Kate Reade. Telegrams were the e-mail of the early twentieth century. Sub-oceanic cables transmitted messages transcontinentally. Cities had telegraph offices every few blocks, and Western Union messenger boys running to and fro were a common sight. Telephones and child labor laws put an end to that.

and launched many a career, including those of Ruby Keeler, George Raft, and Walter Winchell.

Texas Guinan's international reputation as a witty hostess eventually eclipsed her earlier success in Hollywood. When Gene Roddenberry created a bartender character for *Star Trek,* he named her Guinan in homage to the Queen of the Speakeasies. ★★

*Emma Kroebel, the Berlin authoress, in her book recently issued here.*

"Says Mrs. Longworth Did It; Fraulein Kroebel Insists her Story of Korean Incident is All True," *New York Times* (November 20, 1909)

When the cruise sailed into Tokyo Bay on its first stop in July, the American delegation was welcomed with joyful parades, gala receptions, and royal honors. Unbeknownst to Kate and Alice, during their vacation Taft was conducting secret talks with the Japanese that would have far-reaching ripple effects.

On their return visit to Japan in September, Kate and Alice met up with Archie Campion and Boilerplate, who had just gotten out of Manchuria following the end of the Russo-Japanese War. They discovered that Japan's mood had soured—not because of Alice's antics, but because the Japanese felt betrayed by her father, President Theodore Roosevelt. Teddy had just maneuvered the country into accepting a treaty with very unpopular terms.

Frank Reade Jr. was called in with his submarine the *Sea-diver* to protect Kate and friends on the last legs of the cruise.

◆ *Everywhere we go, Papa is now our armed escort. Since fetching Archie and his mechanical man from Manchuria, he refuses to leave my side. They tell us the Japanese are fit to be tied about not getting war reparations from Russia, but gosh!—is that any reason to ruin a girl's fun?*

Journal of Kate Reade (October 13, 1905)

Frank Jr. probably overestimated the danger to Kate and Alice out of fatherly concern. Teddy Roosevelt, on the other hand, underestimated the long-term fallout from his actions. The events of 1905 set the stage for war between Japan and the United States—and for Kate Reade's role in the run-up to that war, thirty years later.   ☆☆

Japanese princesses, "Princess" Alice Roosevelt, Archie Campion, Boilerplate, and Frank Reade Jr. in Tokyo, 1905.

# PRELUDE to the PACIFIC WAR

**K**ATE READE'S **1905** TOUR of Asia with Alice Roosevelt was part of a diplomatic mission that included a back-room deal between U.S. President Teddy Roosevelt (Alice's father) and the Japanese government.

In exchange for Japan agreeing to support American interests in East Asia—and especially to keep out of the U.S.-occupied Philippines—President Roosevelt agreed to let Japan take over Korea. It was another link in a long chain of events that led directly to the Pacific War, the Korean War, and the rise of Communist China.

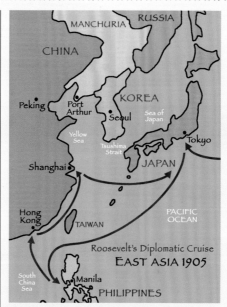

**Roosevelt's Diplomatic Cruise EAST ASIA 1905**

President Teddy Roosevelt sent his secretary of war on a diplomatic cruise in 1905, setting into motion events that would lead to America's involvement in World War II four decades later.

added a new word to the Japanese language: *koroni,* or "colony."

◆ *Japan must keep her plan in the deepest secret, but must make adequate publicity to the people in the world that she is under-taking to bring the whole of Asia from its barbarous and primitive stage to the civilized stage.*

CHARLES W. LEGENDRE, MEMORANDUM TO ŌKUMA SHIGENOBU (MARCH 13, 1874)

## —— COURSE OF EMPIRE ——

**W**HEN **TEDDY** became president in 1901, he encouraged Japan to pursue its own version of America's Monroe Doctrine and become a policing power in East Asia. In 1905, Japan defeated big, bad Russia in a major war and expected accolades from President Roosevelt.

Instead, Teddy negotiated a peace treaty that Japan considered costly and unfair. He didn't want the island nation to become too powerful, after all, and he envisioned Russia as keeping it in check. The Japanese felt they'd been double-crossed. Now firmly set on the path of imperial conquest, Japan would no longer submit to America's whims.

Historian James Bradley, whose father helped raise the U.S. flag on Iwo Jima, lays the blame for Japan's involvement in WWII at Teddy Roosevelt's feet. Bradley writes in his insightful book *The Imperial Cruise,* "It was these events in the summer of 1905 that would doom more than one hundred thousand American boys to die in the Pacific theatre decades later." Japan annexed Korea in 1909 and went on to invade China in 1931. Kate Reade went back to Asia in the 1930s, this time gathering intelligence for the U.S. Navy on Japanese weapons research. ★★

Japanese drawing of the USS *Susquehanna*, which steamed into Tokyo Bay unannounced in 1853 at the head of a U.S. warship squadron. The isolationist island nation was threatened with destruction and coerced into doing business with America.

## —— THE BLACK SHIPS ——

**T**HE FIRST LINK in the chain, Japan's first contact with the United States in 1853, was a rude awakening. Japan was an isolationist country that had been at peace for centuries when the United States forced it open to trade at gunpoint. American warships, painted black, showed up in Edo (Tokyo) Bay one day and threatened annihilation if Japan refused U.S. demands.

This dramatic military display shocked Japan. In an effort to keep its sover-eignty and gain an equal footing with Western powers, the country rapidly built up its technology and military. Many of its people adopted Western manners and clothing.

Recognizing a potential ally that could help secure a foothold in Asia, the United States promoted the Japanese as a superior Asian race that would spread civilization in the region. In 1872, American general Charles LeGendre arrived in Japan to give instruction in how to justify the invasion of other countries. The following year, Japan invaded Taiwan and

The Japanese navy was the dominant power in the Pacific during the first half of the twentieth century.

# ASIAN
# ADVENTURES

*Frank Jr. watches from his airship as a Chinese noble is transported in a palanquin.*

**Frank Reade Jr.**
**AND HIS NEW ELECTRIC AIRSHIP**
**THE "ECLIPSE"**
— or — FIGHTING THE
**CHINESE PIRATES**
(PART 2)
*Frank Reade Library #86*

### CHAPTER XXIX
### *At the Fort*

From the woods there came a line of pirates, armed to the teeth. They reached the rail of the air-ship and came aboard in a twinkling, surging over the rail by dozens.

Pomp was quick witted enough to dodge into the pilot-house. In an instant he had shut the steel door and charged it.

Fully fifty of the foe had gained the deck of the *Eclipse*. It was a catastrophe of the most serious kind. The air-ship was practically in the possession of the Chinese pirates. And Pomp was all alone.

The pirates invaded the engine-room and cabin. Pomp had just enough time to close the steel door connecting the engine-room with the pilot-house. In view of just such an exigency as this, these had been connected with the dynamos, so that by pressing a key they could be heavily charged.

The first Chinaman to essay the bursting in of the pilot-house door quickly repented of his bargain. He was picked up like a feather and hurled a dozen feet away. Several of the barbarians experienced this sort of thing before becoming satisfied. They made vain attempts to get at Pomp, who remained securely behind the steel, bullet-proof screen of the pilot-house.

But the delicate machinery of the *Eclipse* could be quickly ruined by the vandals. Pomp heard them descend into the engine-room. The darky was trying in vain to think of some scheme of circumventing them, when a tremendous explosion rent the air and shook the air-ship from stem to stern.

### CHAPTER XXX
### *Outwitting the Foe*

For an instant Pomp feared that the air-ship was blown up. He rushed with chattering teeth to the window in the pilot-house.

The explosion had given the air-ship a violent rocking. Indeed, things were all thrown about on the deck and Pomp beheld a startling sight. The ground between the air-ship and the wood was deeply furrowed and mangled bodies were strewn about.

One of the pirates had confiscated a spare bomb which had been left

*One way Frank Jr. repelled unwanted boarders was to electrify the metal hull of his airship.*

on the air-ship's deck. He had attempted to carry it away not knowing what was its nature, and had got but a few yards from the air-ship when he accidentally dropped it. That was the termination of the career of that unfortunate Chinaman. It would have been difficult to find enough of his body to make a funeral. Moreover, several others of the pirate crew were killed.

With this crash, all of the pirates in the engine-room had rushed upon the deck. Realizing this, Pomp adopted a daring trick. He opened the steel door leading into the engine-room, then down he sprang.

Pomp now had command of the dynamos and all of the electric wires and switches. It was but a moment's work for him to connect a wire with the steel hull of the air-ship. This was so arranged, with a series of non-conductors, that it could be heavily charged, and only that part of the ship would be susceptible to the mighty electrical current. This was a device which Frank had conceived in case of an attack at close quarters.

Pomp quickly connected the wires with the dynamos and then turned on the current. A number of the pirates were just climbing aboard, when, coming in contact with the electrified hull, they were hurled back with stunning force. Indeed, not one of them could climb aboard the air-ship.

Those on deck, amazed, hastened to the rail. Three of them came in contact with the charged part and were knocked off the deck in a flash. Alarmed, the rest began to beat a retreat. But as quickly as they went to clamber over the rail, they were shocked nearly into insensibility.

Maddened by this result, the Chinese pirates set up a yell of rage and began to throw missiles at the *Eclipse.*

This was the danger that Pomp had feared, but he was equal to the emergency. He turned Lever No. 7, and the rotascopes began to move.

Up went the *Eclipse,* and when fifty feet from the earth, Pomp adjusted the lever to hold the ship stationary, and seizing some bombs he rushed out on deck.

The pirates in dismay had retreated to the cover of the trees. The plucky darky then rushed to the rail. Down went one of the bombs. It burst with a terrific report in the verge of the forest. The effect was fearful.

Trees were shattered, the earth plowed up and the pirates were many of them killed and wounded. In dismay and terror the survivors broke ranks and incontinently fled into the woods.

A wild cheer went up from the fort as it was seen there how cleverly Pomp had circumvented the pirates. **FR**

The Reades' *Thunderbolt* races to help with relief efforts after the Great Quake.

# The
# GREAT QUAKE

The Reade family went on one mission together that involved the United States military, but it wasn't the kind of action Frank Jr. was used to. On April 18, 1906, he received an urgent telegram from his friend Archie Campion in Chicago. "Catastrophic earthquake has struck San Francisco," it read. "Gen. Funston requests immediate assistance. Come and get us with all due haste."

The quake was so big that people felt it all along the U.S. West Coast, from Los Angeles to Portland, Oregon, and as far inland as Nevada. The entire Reade clan swung into action and departed Readestown on the airship *Thunderbolt* within two hours—though not without some debate.

➤ *What a panic! Mama and Papa had the biggest row over this earthquake business. She wouldn't hear of him larking off on his own this time. Once the rest of us found out, it was all aboard. It'll be swell to see Lily C. again. Don't you hate to think of San Francisco all in rubble, though? Only last year, you and I were the toast of the town there before we sailed for Japan.*

Kate Reade, letter to Alice Roosevelt
(April 18, 1906)

## — RED HORIZON —

Even flying at top speed in the *Thunderbolt,* it took the Reades a full day to reach California after picking up the Campions and Boilerplate in Chicago. When they reached the East Bay on the afternoon of April 19, San Francisco was ablaze. With most of the city's water mains broken by the quake, even small fires quickly raged out of control. Mishandled attempts to create firebreaks by dynamiting buildings only made things worse.

The fires were so hot that Frank Jr. didn't care to risk flying over them. He set down at Oakland and readied the submarine he'd brought along, the *Dolphin*. This in turn carried the *Rhino*, a small land rover designed by Frank III, which would transport himself, Archie, and Boilerplate in the city. Archie insisted on taking the robot into the inferno for firefighting duty.

Kate spots the conflagration of San Francisco from the wheelhouse of the *Thunderbolt.*

Evacuated San Franciscans watch the destruction of their city.

◆ *Frankie's little armored car has proven its utility in urban settings. We communicate with him and Campion by means of wireless telegraphy while Father, Kate, and I assist Lt. Freeman's Navy brigades in pumping seawater to douse flames along the waterfront.*

JOURNAL OF FRANK READE JR. (APRIL 20, 1906)

Frank Jr. hadn't planned on taking Kate along with them, but she found a way to persuade him.

◆ *My poor Frank has suffered a second defeat in the Battle of the Sexes. Kate boarded the Dolphin, sealed its hatch whilst Frank's back was turned, then refused to allow him entry until he relented and agreed to let her accompany the rescue party. She is even more mule-headed than her father, I believe. I am certain she will be safe with her Papa and Gramps, while Mary and I tend to refugees in Oakland.*

JOURNAL OF EMILIE READE (APRIL 19, 1906)

## — ROBOT TO THE RESCUE —

FOR THE NEXT TWO DAYS, Archie, Boilerplate, and Frank III helped locate water supplies and fight the blaze. As flames consumed the Mission District, they found a working fire hydrant, three hundred volunteers, and a lone fire crew. The robot and the inventors turned the tide, and the fire was stopped at Twentieth and Dolores streets—saving the oldest building in San Francisco, Mission Dolores.

Stereographic photo of Boilerplate taken in the days following the quake. In an era before coordinated federal aid, Archie Campion felt a moral imperative to help, traveling with his robot to provide disaster relief whenever possible.

San Francisco Fire

Earthquake Series

No. 310. Professor Campion's Mechanical Marvel.

◆ *All during the day and night of the 19th, the citizens and Fire Department, and Professor Campion's Mechanical Marvel, worked to stop the fire as it burned south, and all the time the fire burned on . . . At eleven o'clock water was found in a hydrant up on the hill at Church Street, near Twentieth, and if apparatus could be got up there a chance to stop the fire presented itself . . . The horses were not able to pull the engines up the hill so they were dragged up by the mechanical man and young Mr. Reade's electric motor vehicle, with the aid of the volunteers, and soon a stream of water stretched down Twentieth Street ahead of the fire.*

LAWRENCE J. KENNEDY, "THE PROGRESS OF THE FIRE IN SAN FRANCISCO APRIL 18TH–21ST, 1906" (MASTER'S THESIS, UNIVERSITY OF CALIFORNIA, BERKELEY, MAY 1908)

Meanwhile, the other two Frank Reades, Kate, and the U.S. Navy managed to preserve crucial areas along what is now the Embarcadero in downtown San Francisco.

◆ *It is my firm opinion that the naval force under command of Lieutenant F. N. Freeman, with able support from no less than two Frank Reades (Jr. and Sr.), saved the waterfront of San Francisco from destruction. No praise can be too great for them . . . The ferries, the wharves, the ferry building, branch post office, harbor hospital and coal docks were safe, and to the Navy and the Reades was their safety due.*

ARTHUR H. DUTTON (EDITOR, *SAN FRANCISCO NEWS LETTER*), LETTER TO REAR-ADMIRAL BOWMAN H. MCCALLA (APRIL 23, 1906)

Frank Jr.'s airship *Thunderbolt* hovers in the distance behind Boilerplate in this photo. The robot's inventor, Archie Campion, got the Reades involved in relief efforts.

Bird's-eye view of the fire damage to San Francisco, taken from Frank Jr.'s helicopter airship.

## — ARISE FROM ASHES —

THE EARTHQUAKE and fires destroyed 28,000 buildings, killed an estimated three thousand people, and left half of San Francisco's population homeless. Archie and Lily, who had themselves been orphaned by the Great Chicago Fire thirty years earlier, decided to stay for a few months and use Boilerplate to "aid in relief and rebuilding of this noble city." All the Reades stayed with them, except for Frank Jr.

➤ *My family has elected to remain in San Francisco to serve as housemaids to the city, hauling rubbish and I know not what else, while I return to Readestown to supervise our business and make ready for a new naval undertaking. It is a pity they chose not to join me, nor did they appear to be troubled by my departure. Pomp and Barney are with me as always, yet the Thunderbolt now seems too large for we three.*

JOURNAL OF FRANK READE JR. (MAY 5, 1906)

Kate was stunned to read this passage decades later. "Holy smoke, he missed us!" she wrote in her journal. "And yet he kept leaving. How could he be surprised when we let him go?" ✪✪

## SHOOTING STAR

ONE DAY IN THE SUMMER OF 1908, Kate, Emilie, and Frank Reade III chased a falling star—and caught it.

In the mighty airship *Zenith,* the three of them flew from Readestown to California, intending to visit an astronomer friend of Emilie's, do a little sightseeing, then drop off Kate for her apprenticeship aboard the U.S. Navy's Great White Fleet. Kate was thrilled because she'd been invited to assist Edward Fullerton and Archie Campion, who were acting as the fleet's science advisors, on the second half of its historic around-the-world voyage.

But along the way, the Reade family stumbled into a high-stakes adventure when they got news of a menace from the stars.

➤ *Mama's friend Chas. Perrine, in charge of the Crossley telescope at Lick Observatory, showed us the most alarming images. He has photographed a comet on a collision course with Earth! A mere jot of light, but approaching fast. Mama verified his calculations. Near as we can tell, it will strike the atmosphere somewhere above Asia. My naval duty is postponed while we race to catch it. What fun!*

JOURNAL OF KATE READE (JUNE 15, 1908)

The moment of the comet fragment's airburst above Russia's Tunguska River valley, June 30, 1908.

## — "A SECOND SUN" —

**E**MILIE AND THE KIDS set out across the Pacific Ocean in the *Zenith,* using Kate's wireless telegraphy skills to keep in touch with Perrine as he tracked the comet. On June 30, they intercepted it in the skies above Siberia. Eyewitnesses reported seeing "the sky split in two" and hearing a series of booming noises like thunder or artillery.

➤ *The Earth began to shake and sway, our hut was blown over by wind. Trees were falling, the branches were on fire . . . Above the mountain, something flashed intensely bright, as if a second sun had appeared. My eyes were hurting, I even closed them. It was like what the Russians call lightning. And there was loud thunder. That was the second thunderclap. The morning was sunny, there were no thunderclouds; our sun shone brightly, as always, and here there appeared a second sun!*

*My brother and I crawled out from under the wreckage of our hut. Then we saw another flash above us, but in a different place, and we heard more loud thunder. A wind came again, knocked us off our feet, hurled us against the fallen trees.*

*There was lightning again, and another thunderclap. But the noise was less than before, like normal thunder. I remember well that there was one more thunderclap, but it was small and somewhere far away, where the Sun goes to sleep at night.*

STEPAN IVANOVICH CHUCHANA (EVENKI TRIBESMAN), INTERVIEWED BY ETHNOGRAPHER INNOKENTIY MIKHAYLOVICH SUSLOV (1926)

In fact, the thunder and lightning were caused by the Reades using their electric weapons to vaporize most of the comet before it could do any damage. A chunk of it came pretty close in Siberia, near the Podkamennaya Tunguska River, exploding in an airburst that left no impact crater but flattened eighty million trees.

➤ *I took the helm while Frankie and Mama trained our cannon on the comet fragments, blasting them to smithereens with bolts of electricity. Mama is a cracking good shot, no doubt as a result of squinting through telescopes all these years.*

*We had one close scrape, when the blast swamped our rotors and nearly stalled the Zenith. I righted her by quickly dropping and leveling out. The ground below us looked as if it was covered with toothpicks—every tree for hundreds of miles around was blown down. It's a lumber man's paradise!*

JOURNAL OF KATE READE (JUNE 30, 1908)

A blast one thousand times more powerful than the bomb dropped on Hiroshima leveled a forest covering more than eight hundred square miles.

## — DAY FOR NIGHT —

**T**HE TUNGUSKA BLAST had an unexpectedly beautiful side effect. For days afterward, as the Reades flew back to California, the night skies over Europe and Central Asia glowed bright enough to read by. London newspapers carried rhapsodic reports of "unusual brightness of the heavens," huge silvery clouds, and spectacular colors like "a dying sunset of exquisite beauty" that lasted all night.

Scientists today theorize that the vaporized comet fragment scattered ice particles through the atmosphere at high altitude, forming noctilucent clouds similar to those seen after space shuttle flights. At the time, no one but Kate Reade connected the two events. "Frankie says the heavenly lights are only the aurora borealis," Kate wrote on the first night. "Nonsense! It must be a result of reflective particles from the atomized comet. We've lit up the sky." ✯✯

Frank Sr. during a European speaking tour in March 1912. Three weeks after this photo was taken, he and his wife, Mary, would board the RMS *Titanic* for the trip home.

# A YEAR *to* REMEMBER

**L**IKE HIS SON, Frank Reade Sr. couldn't keep still for long. Even after age seventy, and despite being supposedly retired, Frank Sr. continued to travel and work. At the end of 1911, he and Mary went to Europe on a three-month speaking tour. They booked return passage on the maiden voyage of a new luxury passenger liner the following April, in first-class stateroom B-70.

Mary was particularly looking forward to the voyage and to arriving home in time for the birth of their first great-grandchild, since Birte Reade was expecting.

> *A fortnight hence, we sail from Portsmouth aboard the Titanic in the finest style. Your grandfather of course wishes to tour the engine-rooms immediately upon boarding. Never fear, I will prevail on him to venture above decks on occasion and enjoy with me the sumptuous surroundings. The ship has been likened to a floating town, so Frank and I shall not want for activities to keep us occupied.*
>
> *Give dear Birdie a kiss for me and look after her well in these coming weeks. Soon we shall be gathered all together to welcome your new addition to the family!*
>
> MARY READE, LETTER TO FRANK READE III
> (MARCH 27, 1912)

Two and a half weeks after Mary wrote this letter, the RMS *Titanic* had its fatal rendezvous with an iceberg. The elder Reades, along with fifteen hundred other passengers and crew, went down with the ship into an icy sea at 2:00 A.M. on April 15. One survivor recalls seeing Frank Sr. and Mary that night, although the details of their fate are unknown.

> *After the sixth or seventh boat was launched the excitement began. Some of the passengers fought with such desperation to get into the lifeboats that the officers shot them, and their bodies fell into the ocean. All was confusion in an instant.*
>
> *Mr. Reade did what he could to keep order, and he comported himself with calm as he*

Two remote objects, minuscule against the vast loneliness of the North Atlantic Ocean, are about to collide with fate. The RMS *Titanic* wasn't done in by her design or construction, but rather by an improbable coincidence of human error and weather conditions.

The lookout didn't have binoculars, the overturned iceberg was a hard-to-see "black berg," and a freakish flat calm in the usually turbulent sea meant there was no breaking water at the berg's base, which would've made it more visible. Because orders were given to reverse engines at the same time the rudder was put hard over, the *Titanic*'s maneuverability was canceled out, and it couldn't turn in time.

At that point, the height of bulkheads or the quality of the steel made no difference; the great lady was doomed. Nevertheless, the sinking became a symbol of humankind's technological hubris.

*helped me into a lifeboat. Mrs. Reade was tending to a girl who had been injured. Then our boat was away and lurching down toward the black water, and I never saw them again.*

"TITANIC SURVIVORS TELL OF HEROISM, HORRORS,"
SAN FRANCISCO BULLETIN (APRIL 19, 1912)

Frank Jr. was grief-stricken, as were the other surviving Reades, but tried to take solace in the fact that his father had led "a long and bountiful life."

Two months later, Frank Jr.'s grandson, Frederick Reade, was born on June 12.

◆ *To-day we have cause to celebrate a new life, yet our joy is tinged by the bitter taste of loss. Accustomed though I am to facing—even to bringing—death in battle, the realization that I shall never again hear my father's voice at the dinner table struck me like a bolt of lightning. His sudden absence has inflicted on me a far more grievous wound than I expected.*

FRANK READE JR., LETTER TO ARCHIBALD CAMPION
(JUNE 12, 1906)

✦✦

## MAGICAL MYSTERY TOUR

TWO YEARS after the *Titanic* disaster, Frank Reade Jr., Teddy Roosevelt, Boilerplate, and Archie Campion traveled together on an even bigger ship: the SS *Imperator*. Built in 1913, this excessively lavish ocean liner surpassed the *Titanic*'s sister ship, the *Olympic,* as the largest moving object in existence. It became Germany's most famous symbol of national pride.

The three men were on board the *Imperator* for illusionist Harry Houdini's twentieth wedding anniversary celebration, en route from Europe to the United States. During the voyage, Frank Jr. challenged Houdini to perform a trick that would stump the passengers. Houdini never claimed to have supernatural powers, and in fact spent much effort debunking mystics, but he enjoyed a good prank.

The magician later described his onboard performance in a 1922 interview with the *New York Times*:

On the promenade deck of the SS *Imperator,* June 20, 1914.

Left to right: Luis Senarens, who penned many tales in *Frank Reade Library* and *Boilerplate Weekly Magazine*; Harry Houdini; Edward Fullerton, inventor of the first fuel cell; former president Teddy Roosevelt; Boilerplate and its inventor, Archie Campion; Theodore Roosevelt Jr.; and Frank Reade Jr.

Teddy Roosevelt Jr. was on the verge of a distinguished military career in World Wars I and II. In the latter, he fought with the First Infantry Division (the Big Red One) against German Gen. Erwin Rommel (the Desert Fox), and he led the Fourth Infantry Division at Utah Beach on D-day. In civilian service, T.R. Jr. was governor of Puerto Rico and the Philippines.

◆ *I was asked to give an entertainment, and the subject of spirit writing came up. Archibald Campion and a number of other well-known men were present, all of them having intelligence of a high order. Certainly that was not a credulous audience. I offered to summon the spirits and have them answer any questions which might be asked.*

*Roosevelt wanted to know if they could tell him where he spent his last Christmas Day. I had a slate with the usual covering, and in a few moments brought forth a map, done in a dozen colors of chalk, which indicated the spot where he had been on the River of Doubt. That map was an exact duplicate of one which was to appear in his book and which had not yet been published.*

This left Teddy "dumfounded," according to Houdini. The former president had recently been in South America on an expedition that almost killed him—mapping the unexplored River of Doubt, a one-thousand-mile-long tributary of the Amazon River. Since no one else had ever mapped it and his own map wasn't public knowledge yet, Teddy couldn't fathom how Houdini had drawn the river's exact route. But Archie Campion learned the real story.

◆ *Frank revealed to me, with evident delight, that it was he who secretly gave to Houdini a copy of Teddy's map in advance of the séance. I agreed to keep his secret, as the trick was nothing more than a harmless trifle, and we*

*both confessed to having been roundly entertained by witnessing Teddy in a state of total mystification—a rare sight.*

ARCHIBALD CAMPION, LETTER TO LILY CAMPION (JUNE 26, 1914)

It's not entirely clear why Frank Jr. traveled to London and Germany with Teddy Roosevelt, then left Europe on the *Imperator* just as World War I was about to erupt. Also with them was military intelligence officer Captain Robert Goelet. The Hamburg-American Line, which owned the ship, was closely tied to the German Imperial Navy and intelligence-gathering operations.

These facts, taken together with Goelet's presence and veiled references in Frank Jr.'s journal, point to a possible covert mission during the tense months leading up to World War I.

◆ *Theodore's efforts may produce unintended consequences. Our visits with Uncle Willy and John Bull were full of bluster, and the mood is grim. Had we traveled to Germany in my air-ship, rather than by passenger liner, we surely would have risked its seizure.*

JOURNAL OF FRANK READE JR. (JUNE 19, 1914)

☆☆

The SS *Imperator* under full steam. The square-rigger to the right represents the type of sailing vessel that had carried people and goods across the Atlantic Ocean for more than two centuries. By the end of the nineteenth century, steamship liners had completely replaced sailing packets.

The concept of the ocean liner began with the visionary Isambard Brunel. In the mid-nineteenth century, his innovative steamships—such as the legendary *Great Eastern*, decades ahead of its time—started a contest between nations to construct the largest, fastest, most luxurious passenger ships for the lucrative and prestigious Atlantic crossings.

The Lafayette Escadrille, a French air squadron of U.S. volunteers, was formed just before America's entry into World War I. Named after the French general who played a key role in the American Revolution, the outfit was founded by three Americans: Ed Gros, Norman Prince, and Frank Reade III (standing second from the right). At the far right in this photo is William Wellman, who went on to direct such Hollywood classics as *The Public Enemy, A Star Is Born, Beau Geste,* and *Wings* (the first film to win the Academy Award). Also seen here are the two lion cub mascots Whiskey and Soda.

## The WAR to END ALL WARS

Frank Reade III's customized Nieuport fighter, which he flew into combat from spring 1916 to winter 1917.

ALTHOUGH World War I broke out in July 1914, the United States didn't officially join in until 1917. Frank Jr. was still busy fighting the Banana Wars in the Caribbean, wanting to protect his own backyard. But early on, Frank III saw that the War to End All Wars would shape the international balance of power for generations to come.

◆ *America can't stay neutral; we'll get dragged into this mess one way or another. I am all for jumping in with both feet. The longer we dawdle, the more chance that Germany and the Central Powers will triumph.*

*If our nation will not go to war, we must take the burden on ourselves. Nimmie and I are to meet with Gen. Hirschauer tomorrow and make our "sales pitch" for the flying corps.*

FRANK READE III, LETTER TO KATE READE (JULY 7, 1915)

"Nimmie" was Norman Prince, a fellow aviator who had competed against Frank III in air races for the Gordon Bennett Cup. The two of them proposed to create a volunteer air unit in the French military, made up of American pilots. The French agreed that publicity about such a unit could help rouse martial spirit and push the United States toward entering the war. Thus was born the Lafayette Escadrille.

### — "A FOG OF WORRY" —

IN THE SUMMER OF 1916, Frank III survived his first and most intense combat. For months, he flew missions in his customized Nieuport biplane during the Battle of Verdun, the war's bloodiest campaign. Meanwhile, in the Dominican Republic, Frank Jr. was combating rebels with his airship and ATV.

◆ *Birdie and I keep company together each night to pass our sleepless, silent hours, then go about our days in a fog of worry. When blessed slumber does come, we dream of death and misery. If it were possible, I would forgo sleep until war's end and both our husbands' return.*

JOURNAL OF EMILIE READE (JUNE 1, 1916)

As Emilie wrote this, the tide of public opinion was turning in the United States. It was only a matter of time before America entered the fight.

Frank Jr. decided not to wait any longer. After wrapping up his last Caribbean mission, he went to England and offered the Allies his experience in producing weaponized vehicles. Because he was still unwilling to divulge to "lesser minds" the secrets of his airships, Frank Jr. concentrated on a new land vehicle. The result was the Reade Mark I Landship, which he intended to be the most formidable tank on the battlefield.

Instead, the Mark I showed that the inventive world had caught up with and, in some ways, surpassed Frank Jr. No longer was he the only possessor of armed flying machines, submarines, or all-terrain vehicles. The Reade tank was too big, too slow, and too heavy compared to its rivals. Only two Reade Landships were produced and saw combat.

## — THE CURTAIN FALLS —

İN OCTOBER 1917, Frank Jr. was moping around London, trying to decide what to do next, when he received calamitous news: Frank III had been killed, shot down in a dogfight with German ace pilot Ernst Udet. Deeply affected, Frank Jr. returned to Readestown to mourn with his family.

➤ *No words can describe the wretched depths of my despair. My son's life and my life's work are lost. I am lost.*

JOURNAL OF FRANK READE JR. (NOVEMBER 1, 1917)

Der Gangster Frank Reade Ist Dom Himmel Geschossen!

Frank Reade Jr.—the boy wonder, builder of Steam Men at age seventeen, inventor of helicopter airships at twenty-one—was obsolete. He could still lay claim to having invented cutting-edge electric motors and battery systems, but he had fallen far behind the vanguard. He retired at age fifty-five. And so Emilie Reade lost a son but gained a husband, as Frank Jr. lived out the rest of his days with her by his side. ☆☆

German propaganda poster celebrating the death of Frank Reade III. The German press was none too fond of Frank Jr., calling both father and son "gangsters."

The Reade MkI in France, only a few miles from the western front, 1917. Note the nickname written on the side of this tank.

# WILD KATE'S WILD SCIENCE

Edward Fullerton created the first practical fuel cell in 1893. That same year, at the world's fair in Chicago, his fuel cells powered the excursion boats and Archie Campion's mechanical soldier, Boilerplate. In 1907, U.S. president Theodore Roosevelt invited Fullerton and Campion to serve as science advisors to the navy's Great White Fleet on its around-the-world voyage. Fullerton, in turn, asked Kate Reade to come aboard as his apprentice.

LOSING HER BROTHER to the Great War had a sobering effect on Wild Kate. She gave up her party-girl lifestyle and got serious about science.

Kate continued the family tradition by designing new airships such as the *Aegis*. Her scientific interests also took her deep into chemistry and theoretical physics, toward entirely new sources of energy—or "motive power," as Frank Jr. would have said.

In 1921, Kate was invited by her old mentor Edward Fullerton to work for the U.S. Navy again, doing energy research at a facility near the Office of Naval Intelligence (ONI) in Maryland. She gladly accepted, writing in her journal, "Frankie did his part, now it's time I did mine. The atom is the next frontier in powering the world."

Walter Russell's spiral periodic table inspired Kate to discover deuterium and nihlium.

## — BEYOND HYDROGEN —

FULLERTON WAS EXPLORING far-out frontiers during this time, using electrostatic pulses and rotating magnetic fields to convert oxygen into nitrogen or hydrogen, and vice versa. This inexpensive, efficient method of producing a hydrogen-based fuel was later reproduced at a Westinghouse laboratory by theorist Walter Russell, but was never commercially developed.

Russell also created his own unique, spiral-shaped periodic table that left room for unknown chemical elements lighter than hydrogen. In seeking these elusive elements, Kate discovered what she called *diplogen,* which came to be known as *deuterium*—aka *heavy hydrogen,* currently used in nuclear reactors and biochemistry.

Although Kate made this discovery in 1929, her colleagues were skeptical about it until two years later, when Harold Urey at Columbia University confirmed her findings. By then, she had already resolved to keep her next major discovery to herself.

➤ *Those same all-knowing boneheads will never believe me about nihlium either. I'm going to marshal more evidence and put it into application before I spring the news on anyone else. Keep this under your hat for now.*

KATE READE, LETTER TO ARCHIBALD CAMPION
(JULY 21, 1930)

---

# WALTER RUSSELL

## 1871 – 1963

INVENTOR NIKOLA TESLA suggested that Walter Russell's work be locked away for a thousand years, until mankind was capable of understanding it. Not Russell's paintings, sculpture, architecture, poetry, or musical compositions, but his ideas about chemistry and physics.

Russell created a new way to classify the chemical elements, an alternative to the standard periodic table. He arranged the elements on a scale of nine octaves, in the form of a spiral, the universal shape seen in everything from galaxies to DNA. The depiction resembles the notes of an ascending musical scale, placing carbon as the balance point at the fourth octave.

His model predicted the discovery of hydrogen isotopes, as well as the radioactive elements neptunium and pluto-nium at the other end of the scale. It also postulated that elements existed below hydrogen, in three "inaudible" atomic octaves involving wavelengths that our science couldn't yet detect. Similarly, French scientist Charles Janet's helical periodic table envisioned an "element zero" and, on the other side of it, a table of elements with negative atomic numbers.

Russell's theories are still not widely accepted in the scientific community, but his visual expression of them has a compelling grace and symmetry that have won him many adherents. Some of the strange-sounding ideas he propounded are similar to concepts put forth decades later in quantum physics, string theory, and other branches of theoretical physics. ★★

Kate's journal and other papers from the 1920s through 1937 are incomplete, likely redacted by ONI. Although much of the personal information is intact, the scientific information is not. They contain no detailed information about nihlium. The only other reference to nihlium is in the few surviving notes of Charles Dellschau, an aeronautic draftsman for Readeworks, who also noted it as "NB or neutral buoyancy gas." The Reade family's descendants have tried to find out more, thus far unsuccessfully.

➤ *Please be advised that the documents you seek are being withheld in full pursuant to 5 U.S.C. §552(b)(1), which pertains to information that is properly classified as secret in the interest of national security. There is no information which is reasonably segregable for release.*

U.S. NAVY, OFFICE OF NAVAL INTELLIGENCE, LETTER TO FREDERICK READE III (MAY 15, 1998)

✪ ✪

Kate's *Aegis* arrives at Chicago's Dearborn Station in the 1920s. Within a few decades, railroads would be superseded by cars, trucks, and airplanes as primary transport for passengers and cargo.

The *Italia* reached the North Pole safely but crashed on the return flight, triggering the world's first international rescue effort. The events of the ill-fated polar expedition were dramatized in a 1969 film starring Sean Connery called *The Red Tent.*

Kate's airship *Aegis,* en route to the North Pole to rescue survivors of the *Italia* expedition, 1928.

# RESCUE *at the* TOP *of the* WORLD

**K**ATE READE put her helicopter airship the *Aegis* to good use in 1928, when she and Frank Jr. went on a mission to the North Pole to rescue the crew of another kind of airship—the dirigible *Italia.*

Italian aeronautical engineer Umberto Nobile built the *Italia* to reach the North Pole. On May 24, he achieved his goal. But the *Italia* lost altitude while flying back to base, sinking until its control gondola struck the ice and was ripped away from the dirigible envelope. Without the gondola's weight, the envelope lifted off again and floated away, carrying six crewmen into oblivion.

Nobile and eight of his crew survived the crash but were left stranded on the polar ice.

Thankfully, they had a working radio and survival supplies. When news of their plight got out, adventurers from eight different countries converged on the Pole. It was an unprecedented international rescue effort. According to Kate's journal, Frank Jr. was reluctant to join in at first because "there was no fighting or treasure to be had."

Unfortunately there was also no one in charge, so no coordination of resources. On top of that, the would-be rescuers were bedeviled by bad luck. Roald Amundsen, famed as the first man to reach the South Pole, disappeared during the search. After the *Italia*'s survivors were finally spotted by plane on June 20, drifting on an ice floe, the first attempt to air-drop provisions failed. Then a Swedish pilot managed to land on the ice and rescue Nobile, but crashed when he went back to pick up more men. That was too much for Kate.

◆ *I told Papa that I was going to the North Pole, with or without him, because the "saviors" needed saving before they all killed themselves off. When he heard how everyone else was muffing it, even the Swedes, his ears pricked up and I knew I had him. Papa always gets a kick out of it when an American—even better, a Reade!—can triumph where others have failed.*

KATE READE, LETTER TO LILY CAMPION (JULY 15, 1928)

On July 10, Kate and Frank Jr. arrived at the North Pole aboard the *Aegis*. It didn't take them long to find the survivors, who had painted their tent with dramatic red stripes to make it more visible. When Kate spied their camp on July 12, the chunk of ice they'd been stuck on for more than a month was breaking up.

With only hours to spare, Kate brought the *Aegis* in as close as possible, hovering a few feet above the ice, and lowered a gangplank for the remaining *Italia* crew to board. After dropping them off at Kings Bay, she went on to retrieve two other rescue parties that had stranded themselves during the search.

Kate was hailed in the international press—but her father's pride meant more to her than a world of publicity. "High praise from Papa! He pronounced the *Aegis* a worthy vessel," she recorded in her journal, "and said I maneuvered her 'most capably.'" It was the first and last chance Kate would have to show off her own airship to Frank Jr.  ☆☆

Dime-novel illustration of Frank Reade rescuing polar explorers.

# POLAR ADVENTURES

THE "AURORA" SNOWBOUND.

**Frank Reade Jr.**
## IN THE CLOUDS
*Frank Reade Library #31*

The presence of the enormous iceberg just in their front, with a solid, menacing look that threatened instant destruction to the air-ship, caused a thrill to run through all on board. Professor Grimm held his breath, and Pomp and Barney glared in horror at the iceberg.

But the daring young inventor held steadily to the silver crank that controlled the battery, that moved the rotascopes, and mentally calculated the time and distance. It was short, quick work, and the danger was so great the bottom of the air-ship knocked a quantity of snow off the top of the iceberg.

Every one on board felt the jar, but as the gallant craft soared on higher and higher, they drew a long breath of relief, and knew that the danger was past.

Professor Grimm was almost sick from the reaction of emotions. He had faced a peril that threatened instant destruction to all on board. The danger called up all the terrors that come to one in the presence of death. The escape was as sudden as the peril was, and the rapid reaction of feeling almost prostrated him. He turned pallid in the face, and staggered to a seat.

Frank knew what ailed him at a glance, and sprang forward and caught him by the arm. "I say, professor," he exclaimed, "let's have a drink on that! It was neatly done, wasn't it?"

"It was a narrow—very narrow escape, Mr. Reade."

"You see, you are not used to these things, like the rest of us."

"Are you used to them?" the professor asked, with child-like innocence.

"Well, rather. We meet with narrow escapes very often on every expedition we go on. They are exhilarating. We wouldn't have any fun if we didn't have something of the kind once in a while."

"Deliver me from all such fun!" said the professor, with a dismal shake of the head.

"Oh, you are not young, as I am!" and Frank laughed again, and went out to see how things looked. **FR**

# FRANK READE

## WEEKLY MAGAZINE,

### Containing Stories of Adventures on Land, Sea & in the Air.

Issued Weekly—By Subscription $2.50 per year. Application made for Second-Class Entry at N. Y Post-Office.

No. 25.          NEW YORK, APRIL 17, 1903.          Price 5 Cents.

FRANK READE, JR.,
AND HIS
ELECTRIC ICE SHIP;
OR, DRIVEN ADRIFT IN THE FROZEN SKY.
By "NONAME."

Ahead, Frank now saw a boyish figure in the midst of a pack of ravenous wolves. He was armed with a revolver with which he was firing into them, while he shrieked to frighten them away. Up to him rushed the ice ship.

# INTO *the* WILD BLUE YONDER

Kate on the observation deck of her airship *Aegis,* c. 1930.

I N 1931, Kate learned that her colleague Yoshio Nishina, a brilliant physicist and friend of Albert Einstein, was launching a new project. He had set up a nuclear research laboratory to study particle physics at the Riken Institute in Tokyo. Recognizing this as the seed of Japan's atomic weapons program, Kate alerted her contacts at the Office of Naval Intelligence.

The Japanese military hadn't yet invaded Manchuria, but it was doing a lot of saber-rattling. In the words of Joseph Grew, the American ambassador to Tokyo, it was "built for war, feels prepared for war and would welcome war." The U.S. Navy was concerned enough to build a state-of-the-art facility for Kate at Pacific Fleet Headquarters in Pearl Harbor, Hawaii.

Her assignment was to gather intelligence on Japanese secret science projects and develop countermeasures to any unusual weapons they might have in the works. Placed at her disposal was an elite amphibious raider unit, led by Lieutenant Paul Sinclair, that went by the handle Kate's Commandos.

For the next six years, Kate found herself caught up in top-secret spy adventures, battling Japanese agents from the paramilitary Black Dragon Society and countering the bio-

To assist with covert ops, Kate had a combat squad known as Kate's Commandos, a precursor to today's Navy S.E.A.L. teams.

logical warfare actions of the Japanese Imperial Army's Unit 731. Sparse facts are known about her final mission.

## — A TALE OF TWO PILOTS —

O NE OF ONI's ongoing operations before WWII, now public knowledge, was monitoring possible Japanese military buildup in the Micronesian islands southeast of Japan. In 1937, Kate and Lieutenant Sinclair were assigned to look for evidence of a new weapons research station in the Marshall Islands, which are strategically positioned within easy reach of both Australia and Hawaii.

Kate planned to use her new airship, the *Helios,* to conduct reconnaissance from above. Designed for stratospheric flight at altitudes as high as fifty thousand feet, the *Helios* was a "hybrid gyrodyne dirigible"—a rigid metal airship, possibly lifted by nihlium gas and propelled by nihlium or multidirectional rotors.

At the same time, celebrity aviator Amelia Earhart was circumnavigating the globe by plane, on a route that would take her within a few hundred miles of the Marshall Islands. Kate flew the *Helios* to New Guinea, ostensibly to meet Amelia as a fellow flyer.

➤ *Miss Earhart and Miss Reade are to depart Lae tomorrow, after delays owing to weather and a breakdown at the Malubra wireless station. Miss Earhart, who is accompanied in her Lockheed Electra plane by Captain F. Noonan as navigator, is now facing the most perilous part of her flight.*

"ROUND THE WORLD—MISS EARHART'S FLIGHT; FURTHER DELAY IN NEW GUINEA," *THE WEST AUSTRALIAN* (JULY 1, 1937)

At the Hawaiian base she nicknamed Readeworks West, Kate had a high-tech laboratory of her own design, funded by the U.S. Navy. The air and sea vehicles she used there were also her own creations, but were manufactured a world away, at Readeworks in Pennsylvania.

This photorealist illustration of Kate Reade's airship *Aegis* is extrapolated from the scant reference material available on Reade helicopters. The *Aegis* was scrapped in 1936, and a fire at Readeworks in 1962 destroyed any remaining records. No Reade helicopters are known to exist today.

The *Aegis* was the last helicopter built by the Reades. Kate's final airship, the *Helios*, was a stratospheric craft based on a completely new design. Little is known about the *Helios*, which was lost with all hands in 1937.

An extremely rare photograph of Kate's airship. The Reades are known to have paid off publishers to prevent photos of their craft from being printed.

Amelia Earhart's disappearance occurred around the same place and time that Kate Reade vanished in her airship.

The newspaper's words would prove prophetic. On July 2, the two women took off from Lae—Amelia in her Electra, and Kate in the *Helios*—then headed northeast over the Pacific Ocean. Before the day was out, they had both vanished from the face of the planet.

Despite a large-scale search, no trace of Kate's airship or Amelia's plane was found. The U.S. Navy delayed announcing Kate's disappearance for months, releasing the information quietly in order to downplay the fact that two expert pilots had vanished at the same time, in the same area. The coincidence has nevertheless led many people, over the years, to speculate that their disappearances were related, and that Kate and Amelia may have been on a coordinated spy mission.

## — LOST IN SPACE —

There has also been much speculation, though not nearly as much press coverage, about the fate of the *Helios*. If Kate Reade's nihlium was indeed a gas lighter than hydrogen, in theory it could have lifted the *Helios* into the upper atmosphere and maybe even beyond the Kármán line—the boundary of outer space.

In the 1999 science fiction story "Last Voyage of the *Helios*," writer Kij Johnson imagined Kate "forever circling far overhead, in the frozen blackness of space, trapped between Earth and the stars." Poetic as that may sound, it's impossible. The *Helios* couldn't have traveled fast enough to achieve orbital velocity. Even if it somehow used nihlium as a high-velocity propellant, its airframe would have buckled under the stress.

We may never know what really happened to Kate. Because she spent the last two decades of her life doing classified work for the U.S. Navy, few people noticed her slip into history at the time. With much of her work still under seal, Kate Reade has joined fellow inventors Edward Fullerton and Nikola Tesla as a legend of fringe science.

➤ *Nothing on Earth compares to seeing a sunset from the sky! Tonight the clouds are painted with the most brilliant kaleidoscopic colors—they'd make Monet cry. I'm chasing the sun so it'll last forever.*

JOURNAL OF KATE READE (AUGUST 26, 1936)

☆ ☆

Kate Reade was already involved in covert operations in the Pacific when Amelia Earhart began her flight around the world. Kate may have convinced Amelia to help conduct secret reconnaissance of Japanese military bases, since Amelia's last position was flying toward Howland Island from the northwest instead of southwest.

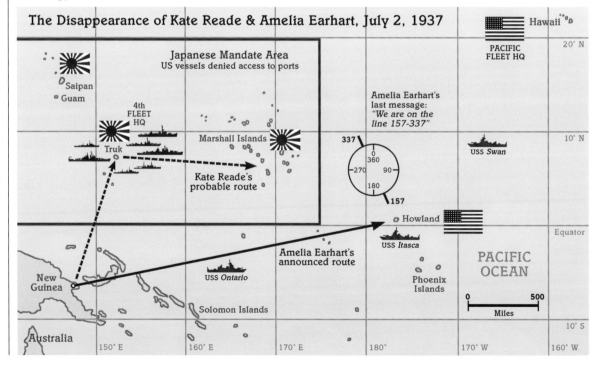

The Disappearance of Kate Reade & Amelia Earhart, July 2, 1937

Hawaii
PACIFIC FLEET HQ
20° N

Saipan
Guam

Japanese Mandate Area
US vessels denied access to ports

4th FLEET HQ

Marshall Islands

Truk

Kate Reade's probable route

Amelia Earhart's last message: "We are on the line 157-337"

337
0
360
270        90
180
157

USS *Swan*
10° N

Howland

USS *Itasca*

Amelia Earhart's announced route

USS *Ontario*

New Guinea

Solomon Islands

Phoenix Islands

PACIFIC OCEAN

Equator

0        500
Miles

Australia

150° E        160° E        170° E        180°        170° W        160° W
10° S

# OUTER SPACE
# ADVENTURES

## LOST IN A
# COMET'S TAIL
— or —
### Frank Reade Jr.'s
### STRANGE ADVENTURE WITH
### HIS NEW AIR-SHIP
*Frank Reade Library #122*

### CHAPTER I
### *The Great Comet —*
### *The Air-Ship*

The cabin was elegantly furnished and equipped with all manner of wonderful devices. Perhaps the most important of these were the chemical generators of fresh oxygen and their distributing tubes. For Frank had announced his purpose of ascending in the atmosphere as far as it was practically safe to get as good a view as possible of the comet.

There has always been a division of opinion as to the material of which a comet's tail is composed. Some learned men had claimed that it is constructed of a train of fiery sparks or burning gases thrown off by the comet in its furious friction through space. Others have maintained that the tail can be nothing but a brilliant nebulous volume without any heat whatever, as there could be no friction in outer space to develop a fierce light.

In fact theories as to the composition of the comet and its tail have been always as plentiful as flies in August. It is safe to say the truth was unknown.

Frank Reade, Jr., declared: "If the thing is possible, I am going to get near enough to the comet's tail to decide of what material it is really made." Worthy object! But what a daring scheme! To say that it was without risk would be folly.

But Frank Reade, Jr., was not one to take back tracks. When he made up his mind to go ahead upon a given course, he was very resolute. He had provided for the possible sojourn of the air-ship in a part of the atmosphere, or even in space where human life could not be supported for lack of suitable materials.

He knew that the chemical generators could supply pure oxygen indefinitely, for he had used them in his submarine boat at the bottom of the sea. The cabin doors and windows could be hermetically sealed, and thus the inmates need fear nothing from poisonous gases or suffocation. It was a wonderful device.

### CHAPTER IV
### *A Change of Plans*

The air-ship was sent upward through the snow storm. Up and up it slowly rose, it being a difficult matter to be sure under such a weight of snow. But soon the falling snow began to grow less, and eventually ceased altogether. The mighty blue vault of Heaven burst into view, frightfully clear and cold, twinkling with a myriad of stars. They were above the storm. Below the blackness of Styx reigned.

The air-ship hovered for hours over the black storm which raged below. Then as a bank of clouds in the extreme south cleared away, Frank gave a great shout: "The comet!"

Instantly all sprang into the pilot house. A wonderful spectacle rewarded the gaze of all. There hung on the southern horizon what might have been taken for a second moon but for the confused radiance about it, and streaming from it far into space in the shape of the tail.

They were at that moment accorded a view of the comet which no other inhabitants of the earth could rejoice in. This mighty heavenly body, which to friends at home in America might at the moment seem a trifle larger than one of the planets, was to our voyagers fully the size of the moon.

It was evident that the comet was approaching the earth at a furious speed. It was yet many millions of miles away, but despite this would make its influence felt on the earth.

### CHAPTER VII
### *In the Comet's Tail*

There was a sudden and instant commotion in the air. The air-ship began to sway and rock violently. The nebulous cloud had, with the swiftness of the wind, closed about the air-ship. It was as if some strange, irresistible element heavier than water had seized it.

Then what followed was for some while only a vague memory. It seemed as if giant hands seized the *Cloud Cutter* and it was borne on into space while utter darkness succeeded. The voyagers were all thrown from their feet by the violence of the shock.

Frank managed to reach up and get his hand onto the keyboard. He pressed the electric light lever. Instantly the whole air-ship was ablaze with light. But through the windows the astounded voyagers saw only impenetrable gloom, broken by vivid flashes at rare intervals.

"Begorra, where are we?" cried Barney in bewilderment.

It was the general query. Frank's face was extremely grave as he made reply: "I believe we are snatched up by the comet's tail, and being carried no one knows how far into space."

A silence like that of the tomb followed this statement. A cold, awful sensation stole around the hearts of all. It was as if all hope were dead, and naught but utter annihilation was upon them.

Connell broke the spell in a hoarse, quavering voice; "My God! We shall never see home or the earth again."

"I fear the worst." Frank stepped to the keyboard and turned on the electric search light. A great blaze of light shot out into the gloom.

Neither did this seem to be gloom, properly speaking, but a dense cloud of dust-like particles. They were swirling and swaying about the air-ship furiously. At times small particles of some matter like pebbles would rain upon the deck or the cabin roof of the *Cloud Cutter*.

It was almost impossible for the voyagers to conjecture where they were or how far from the earth. They simply knew that the air-ship had become involved in the comet's tail and was being carried, nobody knew how far, into space.

On and on they were whirled through the dust cloud of the comet's tail. What would be the end of it all? Where would they eventually terminate their experience? Would it be in some other planet?

Or would they be held prisoners for thousands of years in the trail of Verdi's comet, going around the arch of the heavens long after death had come upon them to claim their spirits?

All these thoughts and theories passed through the minds of the voyagers. It is needless to say that they were in a state of the most intense excitement, and the mental strain was almost unbearable.

Barney and Pomp stood it best of all. They had implicit faith in the ability of Frank Reade, Jr., to bring them out of the scrape safely. Had he not done so before? Could he not do it again?   **FR**

# FRANK READE

## WEEKLY MAGAZINE,

### Containing Stories of Adventures on Land, Sea & in the Air.

Issued Weekly—By Subscription $2.50 per year.   Application made for Second-Class Entry at N. Y. Post Office.

No. 58.        NEW YORK, DECEMBER 4, 1903.        Price 5 Cents.

·LOST·
IN A COMET'S TAIL!
FRANK READE, JR.'S STRANGE ADVENTURE WITH HIS AIR-SHIP.
By "NONAME"

As Barney struck the deck of the sinking ship, the two men rushed to his side. "You came from the clouds," cried the youth. "Roight!" answered Barney, "I cum down from Misther Frank Reade, Jr.'s, air ship."

# END *of an* AGE

After a life laden with near-death experiences, Frank Jr. passed away quietly in his sleep at age seventy.

IN 1932, FRANK READE JR. died of natural causes at his home in Readestown, Pennsylvania. His wife, Emilie, followed him three months later. Their funerals were private events, attended by a handful of family, friends, and dignitaries, including Archie Campion and Alice Roosevelt.

◆ *More than fifty years of Mr. Reade's life had been devoted to invention and exploration. At his death, he was said to have built numerous electric automobiles and helicopters. Owing to his reluctance to take out patents, and to the private ownership of his family's manufacturing business, Readeworks, the exact number and nature of his inventions is not ascertainable. Mr. Reade is best known as the title character in popular dime novels of yesteryear, published under the banner* **Frank Reade Library** *and* **Frank Reade Weekly.**

"FRANK READE, JR., DIES; NOTED INVENTOR AND ADVENTURER, 70," *NEW YORK TIMES* (AUGUST 21, 1932)

Looking back on his life, Frank Jr. expressed only one regret. The last line of his journal reads simply, "I was too often distant."

After writing these words, he locked them away with his other papers in the "stout, ancient wooden trunk" that only his daughter would be able to unseal. Kate Reade inherited Readeworks and, with it, a chance to discover the lost history of her extraordinary family. ☆☆

Two-year-old Frank Reade Jr. is on the far right in this photo of a shooting party on safari in Texas, 1864. Many hunters from Europe, royalty among them, trekked to the American frontier to hunt buffalo. Soon after this photo was taken, Frank Jr. would be lost to his parents.

# BORN AGAIN

LONG AFTER Kate Reade's disappearance, when most of her personal papers were declassified, her final journal entries revealed a secret that Frank Reade Jr. and his parents had kept to their graves.

◆ *Holy smoke! I found a hidden cache of papers that explains events of 1864. The missing piece of the puzzle. Now I understand why Papa kept on chasing Injuns.*

JOURNAL OF KATE READE (JUNE 4, 1936)

Among the last stash of letters and journals was a missive from one of Mary Reade's English cousins.

◆ *We are to travel through Texas after all on our tour of your country—Binny has his heart set on bagging one of those bison we've read so much about. It would be most agreeable if you were to pay us a visit there with your little son.*

ELIZABETH BINNINGTON, LETTER TO MARY READE (OCTOBER 1, 1864)

## — THE FIRST BATTLE OF — ADOBE WALLS

THE CIVIL WAR battlefields seemed so far away that Mary didn't think twice about taking two-year-old Frank Jr. along to meet up with her cousin in the Texas panhandle. She forgot about the other war the United States was fighting: the Indian Wars.

At the same time that Mary and Frank Jr. were visiting Elizabeth, U.S. Cavalry forces commanded by Colonel Christopher "Kit" Carson attacked a nearby Kiowa village. When the Kiowa and Comanche counterattacked, Carson holed up at Adobe Walls—the very same site where Frank Jr. went to fight Indians ten years later.

Massively outnumbered by Kiowa and Comanche warriors, hampered by snow, Carson and his men barely managed to escape with the aid of two howitzer guns. Unfortunately, Mary's party got caught in the crossfire, and Frank Jr. got separated from them.

The following week, a young boy's body was found miles away, at the bottom of a canyon, his features mangled beyond recognition. He was presumed to be Frank Jr.

*The newspapers say our boy is dead. They are too callous, too careless of a mother's heart. We shall search all of Texas for Frank and hold out hope until . . . until we find him. I dare not put words to my darkest thoughts, lest they become fact.*

JOURNAL OF MARY READE (DECEMBER 6, 1864)

Convinced that their son was still alive, Frank Sr. and Mary continued to search for him. After two years of heartrending, fruitless effort, they finally decided to leave St. Louis and start over in eastern Pennsylvania. Frank Sr. founded Readeworks and built it into a bustling business. He and Mary started building a new life together, but the loss of Frank Jr. cast a long shadow on their lives.

## — "LITTLE BILLY" —

MEANWHILE, the United States military was still fighting Native Americans. In 1866, near the region where Frank Jr. had gone missing, the Fourth U.S. Cavalry attacked a small Apache village in retaliation for a Comanche raid. Among the surviving Apache children was an unexpected sight.

*In that village was a white boy captured by the savages. A more pitiful figure I have not seen. His identity is unknown to us and he can not say his true name—the language of his birth has deserted him—so the men have taken to calling him "Little Billy." Col. Carleton says he will learn the boy to talk right.*

LIEUTENANT SAMUEL D. SEGLIN, LETTER TO TRUDY SEGLIN (SEPTEMBER 28, 1866)

No one knows how exactly, but an Apache family had found Frank Jr. and raised him for almost two years. Then his life was turned inside out again when this new family was killed. For the next two years, Frank Jr. lived with Lieutenant Colonel James Henry Carleton, a hardened veteran of the Civil War and the Indian Wars. Carleton had a big impact on the boy, shaping his attitudes about race and power.

*The boy often cries out in terror in his sleep, presumably tormented by visions of the depredations committed by his Apache captors. He is readily comforted when I remind him of the brave soldiers who protect him from getting stolen away by the Injuns.*

JOURNAL OF JAMES H. CARLETON (MARCH 7, 1867)

Kit Carson was one of many American folk heroes, such as Daniel Boone, who made their reputations as Indian fighters.

Lt. Col. James Henry Carleton, Kit Carson's commander, raised Frank Reade Jr. for two years. Carleton used harsh tactics against Native Americans, such as ordering the forced march of eight thousand Navajo from Arizona to New Mexico through a killing snowstorm.

Frank Reade is discovered living with the Apache, 1866.

Portrait of the Reade family by Charles Dana Gibson, 1900. Left to right: Frank Sr., Mary, Kate, Frank Jr., Frank III, Emilie.

In 1868, the *Texas Star* ran an article about "the little White Apache of the Fighting 4th Texas," and one of Frank Sr.'s agents sent him a clipping. Hoping against all odds, Frank Sr. raced down to Texas. He found his son, yet felt as if his son were still lost. Junior greeted his father by saluting and introducing himself as "Big Little Billy."

◆ *I could not bring myself to admit to Mary my abandonment of hope, this past year, that our son yet lived. Here now is proof; he stands before me. Certainly this boy is our son—yet how young he was when taken from us, and how much has since transpired, that he seems a different child altogether. He is overflowing with impossible tales of "depredations" by Indians, yet evidently he was well cared for before Carleton found him. I am assailed by doubt and confusion.*

JOURNAL OF FRANK READE SR. (FEBRUARY 5, 1868)

### — THE LAST WORD —

**M**OST OF HER FAMILY was gone by the time Kate Reade made this discovery—her parents, grandparents, even her brother. She turned to the one man who had known her father best: Archie Campion. *"Why didn't Papa ever stay home,"* she wondered, *"until it was too late? And why the big secret?"* Archie, whose only family was his sister, showed surprising insight.

◆ *Your father spoke of this to me only once, in strictest confidence; but, now that you have discovered it for yourself and he has passed on, maintaining secrecy would serve no useful purpose. I do not know why he wished to keep it confidential, other than that it troubled him to dwell on those years.*

*Frank told me that he hated to leave behind his life with the Cavalry. Upon being reunited with his parents, he could not recognize their faces—they were as strangers to him. He was seized with fear when his mother rushed to grasp him in her arms, weeping, overpowered by joy.*

*Naturally he was made to understand the course of events that had led to this reunion, and over time he grew accustomed to his new home in Readestown. For many years, however, Frank believed it inevitable that he would be taken away to some other, as yet unknown place. Fate had twice uprooted and thrice rechristened him, then, ever capricious, Fate surprised him by breaking the pattern.*

*So—your father began uprooting himself periodically. He was restless all his days, as you know. Although I doubt he would have admitted to this, I believe he went away so that he could return to find always the same family, the same house, in the same place, waiting for him. For he also confided in me that your family was the "one true anchor" in his life. His one true reason, I would venture to say, for life itself.*

ARCHIBALD CAMPION, LETTER TO KATE READE
(JULY 14, 1936)

✩ ✩

# FRANK READE

## WEEKLY MAGAZINE,

### Containing Stories of Adventures on Land, Sea & in the Air.

Issued Weekly—By Subscription $2.50 per year.   Application made for Second-Class Entry at N. Y. Post Office.

No. 52.        NEW YORK, OCTOBER 23, 1903.        Price 5 Cents.

## FRANK READE, JR'S

### TWENTY-FIVE THOUSAND MILE TRIP IN THE AIR.

### BY "NONAME."

The air-ship was rapidly going down to the rescue.  The bear made a fierce lunge, and all lost their balance, and over the precipice they went.  It was a hundred feet to a deep, dark pool below.  The three hurtling forms went into this.

# FRANK READE

## WEEKLY MAGAZINE,

### Containing Stories of Adventures on Land, Sea & in the Air.

Issued Weekly—By Subscription $2.50 per year. Application made for Second-Class Entry at N. Y. Post Office.

No. 51.　　NEW YORK. OCTOBER 16, 1903.　　Price 5 Cents.

# ABANDONED·IN·ALASKA;
## OR, FRANK READE, JR.'S THRILLING SEARCH FOR A LOST GOLD CLAIM.
### By "NONAME."

Yelling and brandishing their weapons, the Indians made a dizzy spectacle. Every moment they drew nearer. Then what Frank expected came; and this was a shower of rifle balls. They rattled against the side of the wagon.

# TIMELINE

"THE SWALLOW"

**1840**
Frank Reade Sr.
is born in Pennsylvania.

**1862**
Frank Reade Jr.
is born in St. Louis.

FRANK READE JR.

| 1840 – 1860 | 1861 | 1862 | 1863 | 1864 | 1865 | 1866 | 1867 | 1868 | 1869 | **1870** | 1871 | 1872 |

**1846**
Frank Sr. is sent to live
with his uncle in
St. Louis, Missouri.

**1853**
Frank Sr. becomes
an apprentice to
inventor/engineer
James B. Eads.

**1860**
Frank Sr. marries
Mary Upchurch.

**1861**
Frank Sr. and James B. Eads
build ironclad ships for the
U.S. Navy.
★★
American Civil War begins.

**1862**
Frank Sr. commands the
USS *Dauntless* in the
Battle of Memphis.

**1864**
Frank Jr. is reported dead
after the First Battle of
Adobe Walls in Texas,
but is actually rescued
by Apaches.

**1865**
American Civil War ends.
★★
U.S. President Abraham
Lincoln is assassinated;
Andrew Johnson succeeds him.

**1866**
Frank Sr. and Mary
go back to Pennsylvania,
where he founds Readeworks
and makes portable
steam engines.
★★
Frank Jr.'s Apache family
is killed; he is adopted by
Lt. Col. James Henry Carleton
of the Fourth Texas Cavalry.

**1868**
Readestown, Pennsylvania
is incorporated.
★★
Frank Jr. is found,
thanks to a *Texas Star* article,
and brought to Readestown
to live with his parents.
★★
Frank Sr. and his son
go to New Jersey to see
Zadoc Dederick demonstrate
the first Steam Man.
★★
Frank Jr. helps his father
build the steamship *Bellona*.

**1869**
Frank Sr. is invited to
Promontory Summit for the
driving of the Golden Spike
to link the nation's first
transcontinental railroad.
★★
Ulysses S. Grant becomes
U.S. president.

**1870–73**
Frank Sr. helps James B. Eads
build the Eads Bridge across the
Mississippi River.

THE SEARCH ABOVE WATER.

**1882**
Frank Reade III
is born in Readestown.

**1884**
Kate Reade is born
in Readestown.

| 1873 | 1874 | 1875 | 1876 | 1877 | 1878 | 1879 | **1880** | 1881 | 1882 | 1883 | 1884 | 1885 | 1886 | 1887 |
|------|------|------|------|------|------|------|------|------|------|------|------|------|------|------|

### 1873–83
Frank Sr. assists
with construction of the
Brooklyn Bridge, on and off
during various stages.

### 1874
Frank Jr. runs away to
Texas and fights alongside
Bat Masterson in the
Second Battle of Adobe Walls.

★★

Frank Sr. finds his son at a
saloon in Dodge City, Kansas,
then sends him to be
"civilized" in London.

### 1875
Frank Jr. meets Pompei DuSable
and Barney O'Shea at school
in London.

### 1876
Frank Jr. comes home, bringing
Pompei and Barney with him,
then goes to Chicago to
study electricity.

★★

Electric Bob joins Readeworks
as an apprentice.

★★

Frank Jr. goes back to
Readestown and works on
inventions with his father; they
exhibit Steam Man Mark II and
Steam Horse at the Centennial
Exhibition in Philadelphia.

★★

Jack Wright meets Frank Sr.
at the Centennial Exhibition
and is hired on the spot.

★★

U.S. President Ulysses Grant
calls up Frank Reade Sr.'s
electric gunboat the *Centennial*
to protect Washington, D.C.,
during violent outbreaks after the
disputed presidential election.

### 1877
Rutherford B. Hayes
becomes U.S. president in the
Great Compromise, following
election of 1876.

### 1879
Frank Jr., at seventeen,
builds the Steam Man Mark III.

★★

Luis Senarens attends
Frank Jr.'s Steam Man III demo
and later proposes a dime-novel
series about the Reades.

### 1879–81
Frank Sr. and Frank Jr. help
Henry Gorringe move
Cleopatra's Needle, an ancient
obelisk, from Egypt to
New York City.

### 1881
Frank Jr. marries Emilie Alden
and builds the electric
land rover *Valiant*.

★★

Frank Sr. searches for survivors
of the lost USS *Jeannette*
near the North Pole.

### 1882
*Frank Reade Library* #1
is published.

★★

Frank Jr. deploys
the *Valiant* in Egypt during
the Anglo-Egyptian War,
aka the Urabi Revolt;
in Alexandria, he encounters
Lt. Littleton Waller,
U.S. Marines.

### 1883
Frank Jr. joins
Gen. George Crook's expedition
in Arizona and Mexico in an
attempt to capture Geronimo;
mountainous terrain proves too
jagged for the *Valiant*.

★★

Frank Sr., Mary, Emilie, and
baby Frank III are honored guests
at the opening of the
Brooklyn Bridge.

★★

Frank Jr. successfully tests
the world's first helicopter in
Readestown.

★★

Standard time is adopted
by railroads across the
United States.

### 1884
Frank Jr. builds his first
electric helicopter airship,
the *Zephyr*, and begins work
on his second, the *Zenith*.

★★

Frank Sr. proposes
his Broadway "subway,"
a double-decker street system
that is considered in
New York City but never built.

★★

Geronimo surrenders to
Gen. Crook.

### 1885
Frank Jr. invents the
Electric Man; Archie Campion
visits to see it; Frank Jr. refuses
Archie's offer of collaboration.

★★

Frank Jr. takes the Electric Man
on a mining expedition in
Australia.

★★

Frank Jr. uses the *Valiant* to
help suppress a Panamanian
revolution in Colombia,
his first mission as a private
contractor to the U.S. Navy's
new Office of Naval Intelligence
(ONI).

★★

Geronimo goes on the run again.

★★

Grover Cleveland becomes
U.S. president.

### 1885–86
Frank Sr. helps build the
Statue of Liberty in New York.

### 1886
Frank Jr. is present during the
Haymarket Riot in Chicago,
inspiring a story in *Frank Reade
Library* #49 in which he is
mistakenly arrested as an
anarchist.

★★

Frank Sr. collaborates with his
son to build the Electric Horse.

★★

Frank Jr. and his airship *Zephyr*
join Gen. Nelson Miles's
Apache-hunting expedition in
Arizona and Mexico; the *Zephyr*
helps pin down Geronimo,
who is captured for the final time
and exiled to Florida.

FRANK READE JR.
IN 1890.

THE ELECTRIC HORSE

### 1887–88

The Reades spend time in Europe while Frank Sr. helps build the Eiffel Tower.

★★

Frank Jr. treks through the Congo in Africa to find Henry M. Stanley's lost Emin Pasha Relief Expedition.

### 1889

Frank Jr. is involved in a German-American naval standoff during the Samoan Crisis, narrowly escaping a hurricane that destroys the other ships.

★★

Frank Sr. aids in fighting the Great Seattle Fire in Washington State.

### 1889–90

Frank Sr. helps build the first long-distance electric power transmission line in the United States, from Willamette Falls to Portland, Oregon.

### 1892–1900

Frank Sr. helps construct the Chicago Drainage Canal (now the Ship and Sanitary Canal), reversing the flow of the Chicago River; he trains engineers who go on to work on the Panama Canal.

### 1893

Archie Campion unveils his mechanical soldier, later to be dubbed Boilerplate, at the World's Columbian Exposition in Chicago.

★★

The Reade family visits Archie and his sister, Lily, in Chicago and attends a demonstration of Boilerplate at the world's fair.

★★

Readeworks shuts down its robotics division. Frank Sr. retires from inventing but continues his public-works projects.

### 1895

Frank III and Kate foil a spy plot on a train, ending up in a spectacular wreck at Montparnasse Station in Paris.

★★

Frank III meets Otto Lilienthal and Samuel Langley in Germany, then starts designing gliders.

### 1896

Frank III and Frank Sr. assist in relief efforts after the Meiji-Sanriku earthquake and tsunami in Japan.

### 1896–97

Frank III and his grandfather help build the United States' first subway in Boston, Massachusetts.

★★

Frank Jr. supervises the nighttime testing of a French military airship in the United States, which sparks a national wave of UFO sightings.

### 1898

Frank Jr. deploys his submarine *Neptune* in combat during the Spanish-American War; possibly sinks the USS *Maine* as a catalyst.

### 1900

Frank Jr. and Kate, flying the airship *Cloud Sprite*, pick up the Campions and Boilerplate from Peking after the Boxer Rebellion.

★★

U.S. President William McKinley is assassinated; Theodore Roosevelt succeeds him.

### 1900–01

All the Reades, Archie and Lily Campion, and Boilerplate tour Australia together and celebrate the inauguration of the Australian Commonwealth.

### 1901–02

Frank Jr. and Frank III build vehicles side by side in Readestown.

### 1901–05

Wild Kate gets her nickname at Bryn Mawr College; she meets Alice Roosevelt through Lily Campion.

THE "EEL"

THE "SEARCHER" STOPPED BY THE ICE AVALANCHE.

IN THE BLACK MOGUL'S LAND

THE "HAWK" WEDGED IN BETWEEN TWO ROCKS.

**1902–03**

Frank Jr. torpedoes a German Imperial Navy ship to break the blockade of Venezuela.

**1903**

Frank Jr. and U.S. Marines support Panama's rebellion against Colombia, so that the United States can build the Panama Canal.
★★
Frank Jr. and Maj. Smedley Butler rescue the American ambassador during a revolution in Honduras.

**1904**

Construction resumes on the Panama Canal, under U.S. control.

**1905**

Kate travels with Alice Roosevelt and U.S. Secretary of War William Howard Taft on a cruise to Asia.
★★
Archie and Boilerplate meet Kate and Alice in Tokyo after the Russo-Japanese War ends; Frank Jr. is called in to protect them, due to Japanese ire over treaty terms.

**1906**

The Campions, Boilerplate, and the Reades fly to San Francisco in the *Thunderbolt* to assist with firefighting and disaster relief after the Great Quake.
★★
Frank III collaborates with Glenn Curtiss on airplane designs.
★★
Frank Jr. helps U.S. forces invade Cuba to quell unrest following a corrupt election.

**1907**

Kate meets Texas Guinan in New York City; while joyriding in the *Valiant*, they foil a train robbery.
★★
Frank III forms the Aerial Experiment Association (AEA) with Alexander Graham Bell, then recruits Curtiss.
★★
Frank Jr. rescues deposed dictator Gen. Manuel Bonilla during a revolution in Honduras.

**1908**

Frank III and Curtiss help design the first airplanes to fly using ailerons, the AEA's *White Wing* and *June Bug.*
★★
Kate, Frank III, and Emilie cause the Tunguska Event when they vaporize a comet fragment high above Siberia.
★★
Frank III builds his airplane *Yellow Bird.*

**1908–09**

Kate accompanies Edward Fullerton, Archie, and Boilerplate on the U.S. Navy's Great White Fleet as it voyages around the world.

**1910**

Frank III organizes and flies in the Los Angeles International Air Meet, the first air show in the United States, as well as other air meets around the country; he takes Teddy Roosevelt on the first presidential airplane flight in St. Louis, Missouri.
★★
Frank III marries Birte "Birdie" Svensson.
★★
Frank Jr. and U.S. Marines back up rebels in Nicaragua, ultimately helping them topple the government.

**1911**

Frank Jr. conducts experiments with concussive weapons in the Arctic, causing a record cold snap and violent storms that sweep through the United States on November 11, 1911.
★★
Frank Sr. and Mary travel on a speaking tour in Europe.

**1912**

Frederick Reade is born in Readestown.
★★
Frank Sr. and Mary go down with the *Titanic* on their way home from England.

**1917**

Frank III is killed in a dogfight with German ace Ernst Udet.

| 1910 | 1911 | 1912 | 1913 | 1914 | 1915 | 1916 | 1917 |

**1912**

Kate and Emilie investigate a large meteorite fall in Holbrook, Arizona.
★★
Frank Jr. and the *Intrepid* help U.S. Marines suppress a rebellion against the U.S.-installed government in Nicaragua; he nicknames Maj. Butler "Old Gimlet Eye."
★★
Frank III attends Archie Campion's fiftieth birthday celebration.

**1913**

Woodrow Wilson becomes U.S. president.

**1914**

Frank Jr. helps Maj. Butler take over Veracruz, Mexico.
★★
Frank Jr. joins Teddy Roosevelt on a trip to Germany and England; they return to the United States with Archie, Boilerplate, and Harry Houdini aboard the SS *Imperator.*
★★
The Panama Canal opens.
★★
World War I begins.

**1915**

Frank Jr. assists Maj. Butler and Col. Waller in the U.S. invasion of Haiti, with the airship *Eagle.*
★★
Frank III goes to France with Norman Prince to propose a volunteer squad of American fighter pilots under French command.

**1916**

Frank Jr. and U.S. Marines defeat rebels in the Dominican Republic.
★★
Frank III and seven other American pilots start flying combat missions in WWI as the *Escadrille Américaine,* later renamed the Lafayette Escadrille.
★★
Frank Jr. goes to France to design tanks and be near his son.

**1917**

Frank Jr. returns to Readestown after his son's death.
★★
The United States joins World War I.

**1932**

Frank Jr. and Emilie die of natural causes in Readestown.

**1937**

Kate flies to New Guinea to meet Amelia Earhart; both disappear in flight days later.

| 1918 | 1919 | **1920** | 1921 | 1922 | 1923 | 1924 | 1925 | 1926 | 1927 | 1928 | 1929 | **1930 – 1940** |

**1918**

Boilerplate disappears during battle in France.

★ ★

World War I ends.

**1919**

Pompei DuSable and Barney O'Shea retire.

**1920**

Kate and Lily help found the League of Women Voters in Chicago.

**1921**

Kate goes to work for ONI, doing advanced energy research with Edward Fullerton in Maryland.

**1925**

Kate builds the airship *Aegis*.

★ ★

Jack Wright and Electric Bob retire.

**1928**

Kate and Frank Jr., flying Kate's new helicopter airship *Aegis*, rescue the crew of the dirigible airship *Italia* and two other rescue parties near the North Pole.

**1929**

Kate discovers diplogen, or heavy hydrogen, which will later be known as deuterium and used in nuclear reactors.

**1930**

Kate discovers nihlium, thought to be an element lighter than hydrogen.

**1931**

The U.S. Navy builds Kate a special facility at Pearl Harbor, Hawaii, to monitor and develop countermeasures to Japanese weapons research; for the next six years, she conducts intelligence operations with the help of Lt. Paul Sinclair and Kate's Commandos.

**1932**

Kate finds her father's journals and other papers.

**1937**

Kate and Lt. Sinclair are assigned to investigate Japanese activity in the Marshall Islands.

**1939**

World War II begins.

THE "FLYING ARAB."

# ABOUT THE AUTHORS

Husband-and-wife team **PAUL GUINAN** and **ANINA BENNETT** coauthored the acclaimed book *Boilerplate: History's Mechanical Marvel*. They've been collaborating in print since 1989, when they created the groundbreaking science fiction comic *Heartbreakers,* an action series that explores the personal and political ramifications of cloning. Their 2005 graphic novel *Heartbreakers Meet Boilerplate* stars Anina as the main characters and was nominated for an Eisner Award for Paul's innovative art. In 1998 they launched their website, BigRedHair.com, which was the birthplace of Boilerplate.

Paul is a multimedia artist and recovering Chicago television personality. He combined his skills in illustration, photography, and model making with his love of history when he created Boilerplate, the Victorian-era robot. Paul also cocreated *Chronos,* a time travel series from DC Comics, and is internationally known as an authority on nineteenth-century automatons. With Anina at his side, he has lived with the Apache in traditional fashion, sailed the Pacific on a square-rigged brig, and walked the sands of the Roman Coliseum.

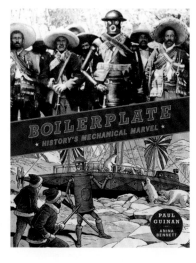

Anina, first published at age fifteen, has penned five *Heartbreakers* graphic novels and edited everything from *Star Wars* comic books to Supreme Court briefs. It's a good thing she loves to travel, because her career has taken her from Chicago, where she cut her teeth at First Comics; to Dark Horse Comics in Oregon, where she collaborated with renowned author Harlan Ellison; and to Denmark, where she handled Mickey Mouse tales for multimedia giant Egmont. Anina teaches comics writing workshops for students of all ages.

Paul and Anina were raised in Chicago and have known each other since before the Internet existed. They now reside in Portland, Oregon, with their second Weimaraner, Bowie.

## — AUTHORS' NOTE —

This is a companion volume to *Boilerplate: History's Mechanical Marvel.* Further adventures of Frank Reade Jr.'s friend Archibald Campion and the robot known as Boilerplate, during historic events such as World War I, are chronicled in that book, also published by Abrams Image.

"Noname's" Latest and Best Stories are Published in This Library.

# FRANK READE LIBRARY

*Entered as Second Class Matter at the New York, N. Y., Post Office, October 5, 1892.*

No. 17. { COMPLETE. }    FRANK TOUSEY, Publisher, 34 & 36 North Moore Street, New York.    { PRICE } { 5 CENTS. }    Vol. I
New York, January 14, 1893.    Issued Weekly.

*Entered according to the Act of Congress, in the year 1893, by FRANK TOUSEY, in the office of the Librarian of Congress, at Washington, D. C.*

# FRANK READE JR.'S NEW ELECTRIC SUBMARINE BOAT "THE EXPLORER;" OR, TO THE NORTH POLE UNDER THE ICE.

### By "NONAME."